RIOT
BABY

ALSO BY TOCHI ONYEBUCHI

Beasts Made of Night
Crown of Thunder
War Girls

RIOT BABY

TOCHI ONYEBUCHI

A TOM DOHERTY ASSOCIATES BOOK
NEW YORK

RIOT BABY

Copyright © 2019 by Tochi Onyebuchi

All rights reserved.

Edited by Ruoxi Chen

A Tor.com Book
Published by Tom Doherty Associates
120 Broadway
New York, NY 10271

www.tor.com

Tor® is a registered trademark of Macmillan Publishing Group, LLC.

Library of Congress Cataloging-in-Publication Data

Names: Onyebuchi, Tochi, author.
Title: Riot baby / Tochi Onyebuchi.
Identifiers: LCCN 2019041049 (print) | LCCN 2019041050 (ebook) |
ISBN 9781250214751 (hardback) | ISBN 9781250214768 (ebook)
Subjects: GSAFD: Dystopias. | Science fiction.
Classification: LCC PS3615.N93 R56 2020 (print) | LCC PS3615.N93
(ebook) | DDC 813/.6—dc23
LC record available at https://lccn.loc.gov/2019041049
LC ebook record available at https://lccn.loc.gov/2019041050

Our books may be purchased in bulk for promotional, educational, or business use. Please contact your local bookseller or the Macmillan Corporate and Premium Sales Department at 1–800–221–7945, extension 5442, or by email at MacmillanSpecialMarkets@macmillan.com.

First Edition: January 2020

Printed in the United States of America

0 9 8 7 6 5 4 3 2 1

For my brother, Chibuikem

1

SOUTH CENTRAL

BEFORE her Thing begins. Before even Kev is born. Before the move to Harlem. Ella on a school bus ambling through a Piru block in Compton and the kids across the aisle from her in blue giggling and throwing up Crip gang signs out the window at the Bloods in the low-rider pulling up alongside the bus. Somebody, a kid-poet, scribbling in a Staples composition notebook, head down, dutiful, praying almost. Two girls in front of Ella clapping their hands together in a faster, more intricate patty-cake, bobbing their heads side to side, smiling crescent moons at each other.

Bus slowing, then stopped. Metallic tapping on the plastic doors, which whoosh open, and warm air whooshes in with the Pirus that stomp up the steps in their red-and-black lumberjack tops with white shirts underneath and their red bandannas in their pockets and their .357 Magnums in their hands, and one of them goes up to the ringleader kid who had been throwing up the signs most fervently and presses the barrel of the gun to his temple and cocks back the hammer and tells the kid to stay in school and if he catches him chucking up another Crip sign, he's gonna knock his fuckin' top off, feel me? And Ella can see in the gangbanger's eyes that he's got no compunctions about it, that this is only half an act, it's only half meant to scare the kid away from the corner, that if it came to it, the guy would meet disrespect with murder.

Ella hates South Central. She doesn't know it yet, but can sense vaguely in a whisper that Harlem and a sweltering apartment and a snowball are somewhere in the distance, not close enough to touch, but close enough to see.

———

Ella calls her Grandma even though she's not Mama's mother. Still, she does all the grandma things. Takes Ella to church when Mama's working or out or passed out on the couch from whatever she was doing the night before. Brings Werther's chewy candies in the wrinkled gold wrappers whenever she comes by to help out with the chores. Keeps the bangers with their 40s of Olde English at bay when they loiter a little too close to the house and the garden that she protects like it's her grandchild too. And now Ella's old enough that she can sit outside on the porch to escape the heat that gets trapped indoors, the heat that turns the plastic covering the couch into a lit stovetop.

Grandma sweeps bullet shells out of the empty driveway while Ella chews on her second Werther's of the afternoon.

Blessing, the pit bull next door, yanks itself against its chain, and Ella shakes her head, as if to say "It's too hot, I know," but dogs can't talk, and this one wouldn't listen anyway. Still, she remembers Mama telling her not to egg that dog on, not to tease it because one day the chain around its neck and the chain-link fence it sometimes throws itself against won't be enough.

One of the neighbors, LaTonya, walks by holding her baby, Jelani, against her chest, and Grandma stops sweeping and smiles, and LaTonya holds one of Jelani's wrists and makes him wave at Grandma. "Say hi, Jelani," LaTonya coos.

"Oooh, he's so *big!*" Grandma tells LaTonya, and LaTonya brings him over, hesitating only a moment to acknowledge the pit bull.

"Pretty soon, he'll be ready for daycare," LaTonya says, and even from the porch, Ella can see the light twinkling in her eyes.

Grandma smiles wide. "The way you look at that child . . ."

"I know." LaTonya shows her teeth when she grins, bounces Jelani a little bit. "Doesn't look a thing like his daddy, but don't tell Ty I said that." And the two women giggle.

"Well, you know Lanie's getting her business started up soon, so you should stop by. She's been sticking sticky notes on everything, and she's been saving up for a play-pen. Even talking with the library about getting books for the kids. Lanie says we'll eventually get a computer set up, so the kids can play their games after school. I don't know how I feel about them staring at a screen all day, but sometimes it's best to be indoors."

"Well, you let me know when it's up and running. Jelani would love to make some new friends. Ain't that right, Jello."

Jelani buries his face in his mother's chest.

"Oh, he's so shy."

The sun feels too bright outside like it's washing the color out of everything, and dizziness hits Ella like a brick. Grandma and LaTonya are still talking when Ella staggers to her feet and stumbles inside, and the light falls in rectangles through the burglar bars over the windows. In the bathroom, she stands over the sink and lets the blood slide a little bit from her nose before tilting her head back up. It always feels like something's rumbling whenever she gets the nosebleeds, like the earth is gathering itself up under her, but whenever they stop, the nosebleeds, and she looks around, it's like nobody else noticed a thing. Vertigo pitches her forward. She leans on the sink, squeezes her eyes shut and tries not to think of what she saw outside: the boy named Jelani, grown to ten years old, walking the five blocks home from school, a bounce in his walk and his eyes big and brown before a low-rider screeches nearby and a man with a blue bandana over his face levels a shotgun out the window at someone standing behind Jelani and, after the bang, everyone scatters, leaving Jelani on the ground, staring up at the too-bright sun for the last, longest two minutes of his life.

Grandma finds Ella on the floor, gasping in a long, aching wheeze, then another, then another.

"Oh, Jesus," and suddenly, she's at Ella's side and has the child's face buried in her chest and rocks her back and forth, even as Ella grows limp. "Oh, Jesus, Jesus, Jesus. Spare this child."

And Ella's breath slows, and she comes to. "One Mississippi," she whispers.

"What?"

"Two Mississippi."

"Child, what are you doing?"

"Three Mississippi." A breath. A normal one, then a heavy sigh. "Mama says, when I get my panic attacks to count my Mississippis until it goes away."

Grandma sounds surprised when she laughs.

———

"Good morning, Junior Church!"

As tall as Brother Harvey is, his suit always seems too big for him. Too many buttons. But it never falls off, no matter how much Ella and Kiana and Jahnae giggle at him. None of the helpers down here in the church basement wear the white gloves the ushers upstairs in the grown-ups' service wear, so Ella can sometimes see the tattoos on their hands. Brother Harvey moves back and forth in the little row of colored light thrown there by the stained-glass windows with orchids etched into them.

"How many of you pray?" he asks in his too-big voice. He sounds like God.

Ella raises her hand.

"How many of you pray every day?" She puts her hand down. Jahnae keeps hers up, but Ella knows she's lying.

"You don't pray every day," she hisses. Jahnae cuts her eyes at her for a second, but keeps her hand up.

"How many of you do things that are wrong?"

Ella remembers that time she lied about putting her clothes in the wash and, instead, stuffed them into the closet she was supposed to hide in whenever bangers congregated in the alley behind the house. And she puts her hand up.

"God says," Brother Harvey booms, "'If you do things wrong and come to me, I'll forgive you.'" He walks over to Kaylen, the little boy three down from Ella with suspenders and a clip-on tie. Brother Harvey's hand rises like he's going to hit him. "If I hit Kaylen here, what is he supposed to do?"

"Forgive you," all the kids shout, except Ella.

"That means Kaylen's not supposed to hit me back, right?"

Ella wonders what she would do if Brother Harvey hit Kaylen with that too-big hand of his.

"Now, I'm not saying Kaylen shouldn't defend himself." He puts his hand to Kaylen's head, cups it. "Kaylen, you say, 'Brother Harvey, I will defend myself, and then at an appropriate time, I will forgive you. And I will do both of these things vigorously.'"

The air starts to change the same way it does whenever Ella catches herself daydreaming, imagining. And she sees an older Kaylen, filled out and all man, working in a hospital as an orderly, and all his patients are old, way older than him, and over and over, the old patients, when they get slow and know it's not going to be too long now, ask him to sit with them. No bang, no blue bandanna, no pool of blood on the sidewalk. Reflexively, she grips the tissues in the pocket of her frilly dress. She's up in the front, and a nosebleed now would embarrass her in front of everybody. But it never comes, and she lets go of the tissues and pretty soon they're singing. Brother Harvey says a prayer for all of them, anointing them; then he sends them back out to their parents or grandparents or people who act like their parents because they need to.

Ella's so tiny that when the ladies crowd around her, their big hats come together like pink flower tops to hide her from the sun.

Mama has Ella's hand in hers as they walk to the bus stop. Ella skips over the cracks where weeds poke through, more of Grandma's Werther's in her pocket. Jahnae will be waiting for them. When Ella looks up, though, Mama's face is drawn tight, and quiet. Her stomach has grown so big that every step is deliberate. And this is what happens to you when you get pregnant, Ella realizes. You can't skip no more.

"Mama?"

"Oh," she says, like she's been sleepwalking.

"Mama, you okay?"

"Yeah, honey. Just . . . I got a lot to do today, that's all. Setting up for the daycare." Then she grows silent.

"It's okay, Mama. I daydream too."

"Do you, now?"

"Mmhmm." A pause. "But when I do, they're usually sad. Sometimes, they're happy like with Kaylen, but most of the time, they're sad." She stops skipping, but still watches out for the cracks. "I see bad things happening to the boys. Like, Jelani getting shot. And after Lesane turns ten, Crips are gonna ask him what set he's from and even though his mama's gonna teach him to say he doesn't bang, it's not gonna— Ow!"

Mama wakes up again and stops, almost like she's just now noticing how hard she's been squeezing her daughter's hand. "Oh, baby, I'm so sorry," she says, kneeling, but Ella's crying by now, wiping her face with the back of her hand.

"Mama, you hurt me!"

"I know. I'm so sorry, baby," and she hugs Ella close to her bulging stomach. "I'm so sorry," she whispers into her pigtails.

"I hate it here."

Mama blinks.

"I hate it here. Everything's so—" She searches for a word that will tell Mama how violent it always is or how much she hates having to hide in the closet every time it even looks like gangbangers might roll through, how she hates having to already know what it means to live in Hoover territory, how she almost always imagines horrible things happening to the boys here and how she can't imagine anything else anymore, a word that will describe the pit that sits in her stomach all the time and the way the ground rumbles beneath her every time she gets a nosebleed like it's going to open its mouth and swallow everything. "It's so bad here," she whimpers.

"Oh, baby." A look of helplessness flits across Mama's face. Desperation, then it passes, and Ella already knows it's because Mama knows she can't let Ella see her hopeless, and Ella hates that she has to know that. "Baby, that's just the Devil at work. But you know there's more out there than just the Devil."

"But everything's the Devil!"

"The Devil is busy here." Mama has taken to smoothing out Ella's outfit, running her hand down her sleeves. "The gangs, the drugs, all the evil that men do to each other here. Sometimes even the police. That's the Devil. But you just gotta pray, all right, Ella?"

Ella nods her head.

"Here, baby. Let's pray, right here."

"Do I gotta get on my knees?"

Mama chuckles. "No, baby, just gotta stand right here. Just bow your head and close your eyes."

Ella obeys, and Mama's voice comes to her hushed and strong.

"Dear Blessed Redeemer. Please protect my baby, Ella, in these trying times. Please surround her in your hedge of protection. Please bless us with food and work, so that we may be healthy and do your will. Please, Lord, cast the Devil out from here, make for us a safe place and grant us mercy on our journey. I pray, Lord, for the little boys that grow up in this world, that you will shield them, and that you will guide them in your ways, that you will build them into big, strong tools for your work. And that whatever you would have us do, you will make the path clear for us. Lord, bless my Ella. Make her strong. Make her smart. Make her powerful. You are husband to the widowed and you are father to the fatherless. And when you are done with us in this world, when you are done with this world, we know you are preparing a better one for us. In your name we pray."

"Amen." Ella smiles and wants to tell Mama that while Mama was praying, Ella was saying her own prayer. And she thinks Mama would be proud to hear it. But, soon enough, they get to the corner where Jahnae is waiting, and Mama lets her go.

"Be safe, baby!" Mama shouts as the bus pulls up. "Grandma will pick you up today."

Jahnae climbs up the steps in front of her, and they settle onto a seat, Jahnae by the window and Ella next to her, looking through it as her mother recedes into the distance. "After she's born," Jahnae says, "your sister's gonna start stealing your clothes. Watch."

"Mama ain't having a girl."

"How you know?"

Same way I know LaTonya's baby's gonna get shot in a drive-by when he grows up. Same way I know Kaylen's gonna work in a hospital and be kind to old white people. Same way I know something horrible's gonna happen soon, Ella wants to tell her. "Grandma can't keep a secret," she says instead.

———

"Hi, Mrs. Jones," a bunch of her classmates shout as they rush past and form their groups and start heading home. Grandma waves at all of them in small sweeps, smiling her love at them.

"You ready?" she asks Ella.

Ella nods, and they walk into the quiet that blankets the neighborhood after the kids have all spilled out of the schools, and some of the teachers hang around out front to whisper worriedly. About King somebody or Somebody King.

"Grandma?" Ella kicks a pebble that zigs one way then zags another, bouncing along ridges in the broken sidewalk.

"Mmm?"

"How come everybody's always fighting?"

"What do you mean?"

Ella shrugs, not quite sure how to make the words fit what she's always seeing in her head, what always immediately precedes and follows her nosebleeds. "I mean, the gangbangin'. How come everybody's always dying so much? They're always so . . . angry."

Grandma's flats shuffle against the concrete.

"Mama says it's devilment. It's the Devil that makes everyone so angry."

Grandma's brow creases in a frown, and Ella wonders if Grandma's forgotten about her because she's got this faraway look in her eyes, and it looks sometimes like how Mama stares out, not looking at anything really but seeing something Ella can't see. "They're not angry at each other," Grandma says finally. "Not really."

"Then what are they angry at?" She balls her hands into a fist like whenever she gets close to figuring out a spot in her multiplication table but isn't quite there yet. "Does it have to do with Rodney King?"

Grandma's foot catches, but then she rights herself. "What you know about Rodney King?"

"I saw some of my teachers watching the video. How the police beat him."

Grandma says nothing.

Ella tugs on her sleeve. "Grandma, something bad's gonna happen."

"God's will is the only thing that's gonna happen."

They round a corner and find a group of boys outside the Pay-Less Liquor on Florence. There's shouting going on inside and things breaking, and before Ella can get a good look at whether or not anyone's wearing gang rags, Grandma pulls her the other way.

"But Grandma, home's that way."

"It's not safe," Grandma says, breathlessly, as she pulls Ella to move faster.

Ella hears the glass of the front door to the liquor store shatter and she hurries ahead of Grandma.

But further down Florence, they stop. All of a sudden, the air grows hot. It's like the quiet from earlier was hiding something. Ella's heart sinks. The ground is going to come up and swallow us, she realizes. Already, at Florence and Halldale, two dozen LAPD officers are forcing a boy into the back of a patrol car as a mass of spectators rumbles toward them.

"Seandel!" someone in the surging crowd calls out. They move like a wave toward the cops. "Seandel!" And terror spikes through Ella's heart. Somebody in the thick of it pulls out a camcorder and hunches his back to start filming.

Ella looks over her shoulder again as she runs with Grandma, and she sees the tsunami of black folks swarm toward the officers, and she wants to be home more than anything else in the world.

Car wheels squeal and rubber burns nearby and a familiar voice shouts from out a window, "Ella! Mrs. Jones!"

Brother Harvey. Sweat beads his brow and darkens the collar of his button-down shirt, and his suspenders are loose and his shirtsleeves rolled up, but something firms up in him at the sight of Ella and the elderly woman walking her home.

"Hey! Get inside!"

And it's almost as though Grandma whisks Ella away in her arms, and car doors fly open then slam shut and Brother Harvey is speeding off again with Ella in the backseat and Grandma in the front.

"We gotta get to the hospital. It's Lanie."

"Oh no, Steven. Please tell me she ain't get caught

in this." Grandma's voice loses its straightness, starts to warble.

"No, it's her contractions. The baby's coming."

Ella in the backseat wants to say something, but she's balled up like the fetus in Mama's belly, her skin on fire and her head a-thunder, and she can barely speak for the pain, can barely hear anything through it. The smash of glass bottles breaking, the sound of gunshots, the crackle of fire, the honking of horns, the cheers, the wails, all of it comes through muffled by the pain cottoning her ears. The bad thing is happening. It's happening, because Mama's gonna have a boy, and she's gonna have it here, and when Ella starts crying and Grandma reaches back to soothe her, anger wraps itself around her, and she wants to shake off Grandma's hand and tell her she's not crying because she's scared, she's crying because she's angry.

"Steven, what happened? What's going on?"

For a long time, he's silent. The hurt that has its jaws around Ella's temples lifts just enough for her to hear him say, "Those cops got off. They ain't gonna go to jail for what they did," and for Grandma to whisper, "God in heaven."

She counts her Mississippis, struggles past four, doesn't get to six.

She passes out and doesn't wake until they bring her to Mama's room at Centinela Hospital in Inglewood.

———

It's Monday when they finally leave the hospital, and some of the people leaving with them come out, injured and maimed by what happened, to find what Ella and Mama and Brother Harvey and Grandma and now Kev find. Everything has been burned down.

HARLEM

STIFLING, suffocating. Even with the windows open, sweat pours, pools, soaks bedsheets through to the mattress to leave stains that Ella's gonna say is just me peeing the bed again. A rat scurries. KEEEVVV! KEVIN DUQUAN RAY MOTHERFUCKIN' JACKSON like an alarm clock. And me stirring on the other side of the room, my fugitive big toe tickling Ella's ear, and Ella swats me away, and it's this and not Mama that wakes her. The rat skitches and skitters. I open my eyes, catch a glimpse, and shriek.

"Ella," I whisper, "the rat."

Ella knows instantly where to look. Without a frown or a squint or even a smirk, she stands, arms tensed at her sides. Then, the soft puff of an animal head exploding. Trails of red spurt out from the shadows. The door creaks open just as the rat's brain erupts, so Mama doesn't hear it; one sound covers the other, but she sees the blood and knows instantly that it'll be another mess for her to clean up but at least Ella didn't do her Thing out of the house.

Rats don't scare Mama, but folks catching Ella doing her Thing scares her, what they'd do if they found out she could do things like make a rat's head explode without touching, that scares her, so she smacks her upside the back of the head anyway. A just-in-case.

Mama shakes her head back and forth but is relieved at least she didn't have to deal with the animal herself, that I screamed only the once and didn't risk waking up the rest of the apartment. Ella catches my look, and conspiracy rides the rails between us. I turn out of habit, so that she can change into her day clothes and I won't see her shame.

Some of the older kids outside the bodega talk about Regents like it's some sort of monster they can't ever hope to beat while the others just shrug it off. And it's this second group that talks the loudest as me and Malik join them. Malik's quiet and confident the way a lot of the older kids are, and maybe that's why Ella likes him so much, and I'm starting to think "quiet" is the most attractive thing in the world, because the girl who sometimes works the counter of the bodega barely says two words to me when everybody's hanging out in the hallways between classes. Ella doesn't tell me why she has Malik walk me back from school every day, but I figure it's because summer's coming and even though gang shit never really stops the heat starts it back up again, like the motors we learned about in science class. Kinetic energy. Thermodynamics.

Somebody's blasting "Dipset Anthem" so loud through their speakers that I feel the crackling bass in my sternum.

"Ay, lil nigga," one of the older cats with Adidas sweats and Tims hollers while the others dap up Malik and talk softly about stuff I'm not supposed to know about. Malik gets me in with this crew, and I don't mind too much, but my bag's heavy with homework I gotta get done before dinner.

"Hey," I say back, wishing my voice wasn't so small.

"Whatchu learn about today?" Adidas asks me. "See this kid?" he tells the others. "Smartest fuckin' kid in the hood, yo. He a cyborg or something. Could fix any computer on the block. I'm tellin' you, this nigga goin' to Harvard on some shit. That's facts."

"In history, we learned about George Washington Carver."

Adidas holds in his weed smoke. "Word?" Then he looks to the others. "Yo, fam, George Washington Carver woulda been that *nigga* in jail."

A chorus of "What!" and "Who. You. Tellin" thickens the air, then they're all doubled over with laughter, and even Malik's chuckling.

"Nigga was the chef up north, woulda got left up north," says a light-skinned cat everyone calls Havoc after the rapper from Mobb Deep.

"He woulda made C-4 outta peanuts. Nigga would throw down a peanut, it turns into a ladder like fuckin' Inspector Gadget!"

They laugh until pain scrunches up their faces.

"They woulda had the wild Peanut Break," Arian says, coughing after taking a puff of the blunt Adidas passed him. "Like, they get to a dead end. And George Washington Carver takes off his shirt, he's got a map of the prison on his back, and it's just the wild allergic reaction to peanuts!"

Adidas: "The COs is chasin' after him, he spreads the wild peanut oil on the floor, they start slippin'."

Everybody mimes a Looney Toon stepping on a banana peel: "WHOA WHOA WHOA!"

Havoc waves his arms to get everyone's attention. "His old lady like, 'George, you fuckin' with them peanuts again?!' and he's like, 'Ma, you don't understand my vision!' You know the scene in *Do the Right Thing* when Spike Lee puts the ice cube over Rosie Perez's nipples?"

Arian jumps in. "HE DOIN' THAT WITH A PEA-NUT!" And that destroys everybody, even Malik.

While everyone's distracted, I sneak into the cool air of the air-conditioned bodega and nod a hello to the bodega cat on the plastic-wrapped rolls of toilet paper by the far wall. It's safe in here, and when I see Jamila behind the counter, the sleeves of her sweatshirt rolled to the elbows resting on the glass with a magazine splayed out in front of her, I know nothing bad can ever reach me here.

"Whatchu buyin'?" she asks without looking up.

"It's me," I tell her, which breaks her away from her photo spread.

"Your friends are loud." And the disapproval is thick in her voice. Her curls seem to hang everywhere except over her face, and she's got those wide brown eyes that make people forget that she can frown straight through you.

"They not my friends."

And Jamila smirks. She folds up her magazine and crosses her arms over the counter. "Ahmed's not here but he'll be back soon. You tutoring tonight?"

"I mean . . . I could, but I wasn't—"

Ahmed walks in, all harried and bothered. "Ugh, I hate when they just hang out there without buying nothing," he mutters.

"That's the neighborhood," Jamila tells him with an accent that's already thick with uptown, even though they moved here not long ago.

"Hey, Kev," Ahmed says before disappearing in the back. "How's Ella?"

Ella's last episode had her falling off the couch and onto the floor, her left arm limp while the rest of her seized up, and wind that came out of nowhere started flinging everything around, the furniture rising like it was being pulled on a string and Ella's eyes rolling up into the back of her head while she convulsed. Then there was Ella coming back to us, just as Mama had finished soaking the blanket in the bathwater, getting it ready for us to wrap Ella in and cool her down while she got herself better.

"She's good," I say back.

Commotion outside. Someone says, "Ayo, put it out put it out!" And someone else mutters, "I ain't puttin' out shit." Then the smack of flesh against flesh, "Fuck you talmbout, toss it. I can't get jammed up again, you *know* a nigga out on parole right now." Then low, familiar voices. Cops. Through the glass, I see the crew all spread out in a line with their hands up against the walls and the windows, legs spread too far apart, then I hear the click of handcuffs closing around wrists and cries of protest and "Officer, we ain't do nothin'" and

I wonder who's going to jail this time, but the cops just wait around while one of the guys lies face-first on the sidewalk, hands cuffed behind his back. Ahmed's watching too, and I see the emotions play across his face: vindication that the loiterers are getting what they deserve, guilt that maybe he's the cause of this, anger that the police are going this far when they don't need to. Somebody calls a cop "Jackie Chan," then there's a thud, and more handcuffs.

"What, you goin' pull out your gun? Pull out your gun!" It's Adidas. "You scared?"

"Ahmed, quick, go in the back," Jamila whispers, then reaches underneath the counter for what I know is a gun.

"You was about to, Officer. You feel threatened?"

I remember there's like eight of them out there, and there might not be as many cops, but some of the cops are laughing.

"Get the fuck outta here, bruh!" shouts Havoc, and I can tell from the muffle in his voice that he's the one on the ground.

"See them laughin'?" This from Arian. "See your partners laughin' at you gettin' straight cooked right now, my nigga? They ain't your homies."

More yelling, shouting, but this time, more laughter.

And I sneak a little closer to the door to see a crowd gathered outside. Backup.

"Kevin, what are you doing?" Jamila in that harsh whisper. "Get the fuck away from the door!"

But I can't get enough of what's going on outside. My body warms with it, like a space heater in my bones. One of the cops reaches down and uncuffs the guys on the ground, and Havoc gets back up as the cops back away, shouting, "You see the address! Come back later, pussy!" And it's not this, but the growing crowd, some of them with cameras, that makes the cops shuffle away. And it feels like victory.

Still feels like victory afterward when Malik comes in to fetch me, says an apologetic hi to Jamila and Ahmed, then walks me back to Ella. The look on her face, that's what tells me today wasn't no kind of victory. That when people joke and call me Riot Baby for being born when I was, it ain't with any kind of affection, but something more complicated. The type of thing old heads and Mama and other people's parents tell you you won't understand till you get older.

———

We're playing on a wooden floor in the apartment. Hot outside becomes suffocating inside. No drapes on the living room window eight floors up, so the sun blasts unabated onto the floor, rectangular hell right in the center, and the room is so small you can't get away from it. Mama cooking in the kitchen and the smoke and smell drift in, so you really can't breathe, but Mama doesn't want me and Ella outside. The heat turns kids violent and she doesn't need a lot of time for her imagination to get to the place where someone shoots and Ella does her Thing, yet uncontrolled, and more people are dead than need to be and Ella's unveiled, or even unveiled and dead, and Mama's left with the pieces and her guilt at not being able to protect her kids. So we're stuck in the apartment: Ella and me, both still kids. I'm sitting across from Ella as she balances a ball of light on her palm, and I stare at it with wide eyes, and neither of us knows yet that to stare at the thing will ruin our vision forever. It glows and black tendrils of smoke surround it, wind around its belly, and steam up into the ceiling.

"Make it cooler, Ella," I ask her, three steps away from begging, and she tries and the temp drops a little bit, just enough to feel relief in our sweat.

I sniff at the food Mama's making and curl my face. "Nigga, did I just catch you havin' fun?" I ask in my best fifth-grade schoolteacher impression, which isn't much of an impression at all, just me throwing some rasp and bass into my tinny voice.

We giggle.

"Nigga, did I just catch you tryna make the room colder?"

More giggling.

"Nigga, did I just catch you tryna make my life worth living?"

Giggling, but I hit something serious and sad and Ella stops.

The room gets hot and suffocating again, and we wait a little bit to see what Ella will do with her Thing, but Mama calls us into the kitchen to tell us food's ready and we don't get a chance. Except, on the way in, I see Ella's got one hand behind her back, the ball of light having turned solid and fluffy and cold, something her eyes tell me she's gonna try to hit me with: a snowball.

———

"Yo, this bud got me smizz off the bliggedy, y'heard?"

I hear the voices before I get to my floor, and I know from the jump that's Havoc and some other cat from my building in the stairwell. I'm two floors below them before I smell it. I hate when the elevator's out, because it means I gotta walk through weedsmoke that fogs the whole place up. You can't even see out the window when they get going.

It's a colder autumn than we've been getting, and who wants to freeze their fingers off while getting high?

"Yo, pass the blunt, though," says the other cat.

And when I get to their landing, I see through the haze that he's got on a Nike Tech hoodie.

"It's poppin' in Brooklyn tonight, they's gonna be mad bitches there."

Havoc doesn't see me coming, but I try to play it like I'm not scared of them. I don't have Malik with me, and even though Havoc has no reason to, he's still the type to sniff fear through the smoke and pounce. They're all like that. Suddenly, my book bag's the heaviest thing in the world.

"Nah, bro," says Havoc. "We got beef in Brooklyn. It's slow."

"Then we out uptown, then."

"Nah, nigga. We got static up there, too."

The other cat's sounding more desperate. "Dawg, let's hop out to the city then. If your hoodie got a check on the left, and it's a Tech, they give you neck, bro."

I can see Havoc shaking his head. "We not vegetarians when it comes to the beef, bro."

Can't stop, can't slow down. So, I walk like I don't

even hear them. The other cat, when he sees my silhouette, reaches for something at his waist, but Havoc puts a hand out to stop him. If I was Housing Police, I wouldn't be moving this slow.

"It's just me," I manage to get out.

And Havoc chuckles, though I can see the other cat ice-grilling me like I'm from the wrong set.

"It's cool, it's cool," Havoc murmurs. Then to me, "You smoke?"

I shake my head. "If I smoke, I'm homeless. Mom ain't got that kind of energy." Also, Malik would kill this nigga if he ever found out I got offered weed when I'm supposed to be on my "stay in school" shit.

"Yo, lil nigga." This from the other cat. "What's it like outside?"

For some reason, his voice paralyzes me. I don't know why I'm so scared of him, but everything just feels ominous. Like the feeling you get when you're about to get into a fight, when all the blood rushes to your face and time runs and crawls at the same time. "What, you mean like cops? Couple outside the building, but—"

"Nah, the weather." What I said makes him chuckle, and he loosens up. Like he knows I'm cool now. "What's the weather outside?"

"It's mad brick out there. I think it's starting to snow."

The other cat rolls his shoulders. "I'm good, I don't get cold."

Havoc raises an eyebrow. "You goin' out with a hoodie?"

"Yeah!"

Havoc shakes his head, takes a puff from the blunt he's still holding. "Oh, nah, you different, bro." He coughs around a laugh. "You gon' catch frostbites, my nigga."

The other cat sucks his teeth. "I don't catch frostbite. Them shits don't bite me, I taste like doo-doo."

"My man, just put on a coat."

I'm laughing behind my fist, trying to keep them from seeing, because I don't know if this other cat's the type to flip his switch mad quick and dead my shit for giggling.

"This hoodie's my coat!" says the other cat. "My coat, jacket, sweater, shirt."

"Bro, you wylin'." Havoc can't stop chuckling now.

The other cat tries to stay serious, but he knows he's playing too, so we all have our little weed-filled circle of laughter until I hear something crash upstairs.

Our laughter dies down, and that ominous feeling climbs back into my belly.

"That you?" Havoc asks, gesturing up with his chin.

Mama and Ella been arguing a lot more lately, and

I've gotten pretty good about timing my absences so that I miss the worst of it, but I can't go back out now. Not all smelling like weed with the cops by the entrance and the snow beginning to fall outside. So I just bow my head and let out a small "Yeah."

"Stay up, lil nigga." Havoc daps me, and, to my shock, the other cat daps me too, though he doesn't say anything.

When I get to our door, I hesitate, then I pull my key out and nudge it open. I flinch every time I hear something break. But there are new sounds that keep me stuck in the hallway. Maybe if I wait long enough, it'll stop. But then voices reach me. Someone trying to talk or scream, but something's choking the words inside them.

My book bag thuds when it hits the floor, and I rush to the bedroom I've shared with Ella since we were little to find cabinets shattered and window glass all over the floor and a blanket wrapped tight around Mama's neck while her feet dangle off the floor. At the center of the storm stands Ella, her eyes glazed over, her teeth bared in a snarl, one hand raised in the air like it's gripping an invisible neck and squeezing.

She's going to kill Mama.

"Ella!" I shout.

I go flying backward into the hallway. A yelp comes out of me when I hit the wall and fall to the ground. Now furniture in other rooms starts to hover in the air. I rush in again, but this time winds buffet me, pushing me back. The storm roars in my ears, and I scream, "Ella!" My fingers grip the door posts. The door is gone, ripped clean off its hinges. "Ella!"

Something inside me rips. Thought vanishes; then, for an instant, I glimpse it. Flashes of memory and feeling like mirror shards. An argument about cleaning our room. A white doctor nudging Mama out of the way while Mama attends to a patient. Someone getting onto the hospital elevator before Mama has a chance to get off, blocking her path. Kids getting handcuffed and tossed into the backs of police vans. Burly almost-police roaming high school corridors during the breaks in between classes. Then I'm back, and everything is calm and Mama's on the floor clutching her neck and coughing and Ella stands in the middle of the room, stunned and soundless and weeping. Mouthing over and over and over, "I'm sorry."

I rush over to Mama as she tries to push herself upright and fails. "Mama," I whisper. "Mama, are you all right?" She manages to sit upright and, with her back against the wall, waves me away, taking deep, shuddering breaths. I scan her eyes, as though to know what's in them is to know what she needs, and I see calm and patience, but there's fear, too. And I want to kill Ella for making Mama afraid.

But then I turn back and I see my sister on her knees, her hands limp before her, tears racing down her cheeks, and I feel it too.

I'm afraid of her.

It's late when I come home.

Even though Mama's still at work, the TV's on in the kitchen, and Ella's sitting at the table, staring straight at it like it's got fishhooks in her. It's not the same blankness she had during her attack a few months back. This is different. I don't think I've ever seen her like this.

"Ella! You left the door unlocked! Mama's gonna kill y—"

Red and blue lights flash on the screen. That's nothing new. News about police or about somebody getting shot, but Ella hasn't moved once since I stepped inside. Her hair is completely gray. Her fists tremble.

I'm about to cuss her out; then I stop and figure whatever she's watching must be important.

On the screen, police tape flaps in the breeze behind the newscaster bundled up in a November coat. Friends leaving a nightclub. NYPD on scene. Fifty shots fired into a man's car. Sean Bell. The newscaster keeps going, but I've only got eyes for Ella, who can't stop staring.

"Ella?"

Tears stream down her face. She's not moving.

"Ella, what's wrong?"

I put a hand to her shoulder. Hurt shoots back and forth between my ears. My eyes shut, and all of a sudden, all I see is fire. People in the streets chanting, people throwing bricks, the scritch of handcuffs closing over wrists. I take my hand back. My palm feels like I touched the stove. But nothing in the kitchen moves. I don't smell any sulfur in the air or feel the ground change beneath me like it always does before one of Ella's attacks.

"Ella?"

"Something bad is gonna happen." Her voice is leaden when she says it. That's the last thing she says to me before she vanishes.

"Kev?"

I turn and Mama's standing in the entrance to the kitchen. The news about the shooting fills the room. "Where's Ella?"

But now Mama's watching the TV and maybe she sees whatever it is that Ella saw, because she's frozen too. And she stands there for a long time, and I don't know what to do, so I start crying, and that's what breaks Mama out of her standing nightmare. All of a sudden, she's got me wrapped up in her arms, so tight and so warm it feels like I'm melting into her.

"Don't worry about your sister," Mama tells me, and she's got that same certainty in her voice as when she's praying over us. "Just . . . try not to be angry. She's just angry, and she needs to go be with herself for a little bit."

"She coming back?" I manage when I finally stop crying.

Mama doesn't answer.

I want to tell Mama about how things were getting better after Ella's last attack, how I've been studying on the side and maybe getting closer to finding out how Ella could do the things she could do and that I'm gonna keep doing that once I get to college and get my degree. I want to tell Mama that we're healing, that we're fixing what we can fix and that nothing's been broken beyond repair and that the only way we can keep whatever's eating Ella's insides from devouring her is to stay together. But more sobs come, and I try to get my brain to move toward a solution, figure out what I can build to get her back, to get at whatever's hurting her, but I can't think of nothing.

———

The Bx19 pulls up janky and almost swerving by 145th and St. Nicholas. I shove past all the bundled-up commuters to find the back door closed. Winter air stomps through the open front door, and I shout. "Back door!"

People mill. The bus idles at a light.

"Back door!" Fuck this. "I know you hear me, my nigga! Open the fucking back door!" Slowly, grudgingly, the back doors unfurl, and I hop out. "Suck my dick!" I shout before tugging the fur hood of my coat up over my head and shuffling to the bodega by the apartment. Already, a bunch of them are waiting outside. I hear someone say, "Aight, so boom," and I'm tight, because I ain't ready to stick around for another hour and listen to this nigga tell another story about how his chick dogged him yet again.

"Ayo, whatup, slime," Tone says, as he daps me. Our fingers twist, curl, and with one last shake, we're finished.

"Whatup, whatup, whatup," until everyone's dapped. "Yo, fam, it's mad brick outside. I'm finna get a sandwich, wait for me."

"Yo, get me a chopped cheese," Melo hollers after me.

"Suck my dick!" I shout back, and everyone chuckles.

Inside is warm, dry air and the sound of good-smelling meat on the grill. Some new Dominican dude is on the phone behind the counter.

"Ayo, lemme get a bacon-egg-and-cheese." I gotta

shuffle from one foot to the other to keep from freezing, even though heat fogs the windows. The dude behind the counter doesn't move, just keeps talking in a low, loving voice to the phone. "Ayo! Can I get a bacon-egg-and-cheese, please." Like I'm not even there. "Yo, can I get a *fuckin'* bacon-egg-and-cheese, my nigga?" I slap the glass to make my point, and five minutes later, I'm back outside, and half the sandwich is gone.

"Yo, you know Jamila's out of school for Winter Break?"

That line cuts through the cloud of conversation, and I forget the sandwich in my hands. "Word?"

"Oh, nigga, that's you?" Melo says around the spliff he's lighting.

"She ain't my girl, but deadass, you try for her, I'ma fuck you up." I half mean it, but I don't know what half they're chuckling at.

A cop car idles to a stop across the way. Melo stubs out the spliff and tucks it in the space where the sole of his Tim is hanging off. There's no other reason for the cops to be here than us, so we get ready.

"Officer?" I say, by way of greeting, but they're angry and they stomp toward us the same way the cold wind stomped toward my face on the bus, and before I know it, I'm on the ground with a police boot on my cheek, and everyone screaming "what the fuck" around me.

My body thrills to it. It's been like this ever since Ella left. Like she took the forcefield protecting me with her. And you hit a certain age and realize the forcefield's a cage, and that's maybe part of why I got snow in one eye and dirt from the cop's Nike boot in the other.

"You got anything that can stick me, you fuckin' worm?" from the cop frisking me. And he almost gets to the box cutter in the inside pocket of my coat, but I can tell people got their camera phones out, so the cops back off a little bit. They got cuffs on me and twist me around until I'm sitting on the ground, and the others are pressed against the wall with their hands against the windows.

"Who I look like, Officer?" I jeer. "What suspect I look like this time? Let's figure this out. Help me help you."

"Yo, why you hasslin' my mans?" asks Cassidy.

I bark out a laugh. "Don't worry 'bout him, he's just mad I hit him with the ill crossover at the ballgame last week. Ain't that right, Officer Ankledicks? So you know he gotta up his arrest quota for the month. Nigga had Sonic rings comin' outta his ass."

The cop cracks me across the face, right on the cheekbone, and I spend a stunned second on the ground before sitting upright and spitting blood into the snow, then grinning through my red teeth.

"Take your gun off, and we can shoot a fair one, Officer Handles. NY Play Dead, nigga."

He's about to hook off on me again, but one of his partners puts a hand to his chest, and the others throw hushed whispers at him, then eventually one of them, a different one, comes over and unlocks my cuffs.

"Thank you, Officer," I tell this one, nodding my appreciation. Then, as they retreat, "Have a good night, Officers! Stay warm!"

When the cars peel off I mutter, "Bitch-ass nigga." And turn around to see my sandwich on the ground. Flattened under a Nike boot print.

———

When I look back, I'll know it's during Winter Break for schools because when I stumble down the street and hit my hip on a trashcan rounding a corner, I'll nearly slip and fall in dirty-ass snow. I'll remember just in time to take off my ski mask and stuff it deep into the garbage, then ditch my blood-spotted coat in an alley before nearly smashing through the door to the bodega. I'm shivering in my gray Tech hoodie, and slow to a stop as soon as I'm inside, wandering down the aisle to the back of the store to see if any blood's gotten on my hoodie or the shirt underneath. Check my face in the glass doors over the sodas. Then the jingle of the bell as two cops come in, and I put my hood up and wander, pretend like I'm just browsing while I make my way back to the front, but the cops are still talking bullshit, so I have to walk back and wait, then try to avoid the one that peels off to do a circuit of the store. And when the blood stops pounding in my ears, I'll hear faint echoes of a familiar voice. But then, I'll see an opening and make a dash for the door, and one of the cops will slam into me and pin me against the counter, my face smashing into the top while they hit me twice in the ribs and twist my arms behind me and the other one raises my head and slams it into the glass again so hard it cracks and blood spills out of the cut above my eye.

I'll know it's Winter Break, because I'll fight against the cop's grip to raise my head and I'll see Jamila standing there behind the counter, brown eyes wide with horror.

In that moment, I'll feel a part of the universe split off, like a branch snapped off a tree trunk, and that piece of the universe has me in it with her. I'm standing in front of the counter, and Jamila's back from Winter Break, and I'm on Winter Break too, because I've been busy at school learning things and building things, and we'll talk about the things people talk about when they know already that they're gonna fall in love and get married and raise beautiful, brilliant, peaceful fucking kids.

But right now, I just wish she didn't fucking recognize me. I'd give anything for her not to have fucking recognized me.

———

One Christmas when we were kids, Mama, seeing what white families got their kids when she would clean their houses between hospital shifts, brought home a shiny train set. Miniature gears and pistons, no chips in the blue and red paint that coated the front car. I would make the chug-chug sounds when running them over the carpet and up the spiral tracks that circled the play-mountain at the end of the course. They'd get to the top, then roll back down, cars crashing into each other, jack-knifing, until the whole thing was a tangled mess at the end, imaginary passengers all crying out for help before the whole thing would magically explode and there'd be no one left to cry out. But one time, Ella told me that the train was transporting dynamite to blow up some bridge that existed in some other train set, and she claimed there was a boy, maybe my age, who had been playing with a lit stick, and instead of metal and plastic, the train cars were made out of wood, and the kid had dropped his stick and was running back through the cars like in the movies, climbing a ladder to the top and daringly jumping from car to car. Movie trailer music thumped in our heads. And fire, real fire, broke out in one car as Ella moved the trains up the mountain with her Thing, the first car puffing into a ball of flames and the others blowing up too until there was nothing but a trail of fire winding its way up the mountain, imaginary wind blowing the flames back like a wave of orange-red hair. It was beautiful until Mama came in, smelling smoke, and ordered us both to put it out or Ella would burn the whole place down and it'd be us kids crying out.

Ella had spent the next year, under my watchful eye, trying to put it all back together, trying to un-char the mountain and re-form the train cars. She never did get it all back to how it'd been, not that either of us could see.

RIKERS

ELLA huffs as she hefts her bag deeper and deeper into the desert. She's getting better at Traveling, but pinpointing locations far enough from people is still too high a bar to vault. Soon, though, she stops and tosses the bag to the ground. Dust erupts in a cloud around it. The flap of the bag opens on its own and out spin clear, lenticular discs containing ball bearings. They come out in an arc until they form a column she has to crane her neck to see. A shoulder-width circle etches itself into the dirt in front of her. She likes it out here, and if someone were to ask her why, she'd, half joking, tell them it's because she can practice breaking things without hurting anyone. Out here with the rusted and abandoned military armament, the detached members and wings of aerial mobile suits and crabtanks and Guardians tall as apartment buildings lying like bones bleaching in the sun, she can pulverize and tear and shatter and not spill a drop of blood. But, really, it's because of the contagion.

She can't stand to have their thoughts bleed into hers, to feel their insides and to hear their prejudice and their hate and their apathy pinball behind her eyes.

She raises her hand, grips a pinch of air between her fingers, then throws her hand down, as though she were pulling a cord under a trapdoor.

The bearings fly to the earth. The discs' pieces scatter upon impact, darting toward the edge of the circle, where they freeze. For a second, Ella wonders if she froze not just the ball bearings but the whole world, too. A condor flaps its wings overhead. Dung beetles scuttle over rocks. The world still moves. She flicks her wrist, and the broken thing's parts fly back together in a perfect reconstruction. After a beat, she steps back.

The column sweeps down to her eye level. She squints. The ball bearings rotate before her eyes. She frowns at the hairline fracture in one of the discs.

The bearings swim back into her pack.

A few bounding steps send her miles deeper into the desert, and she stops at the cliff's edge. It overlooks the mesa, cracked clay, drained and baked, patches of desert floor covered in dust and rubblestone. The wind here whips her silver braids about her face. This is always her favorite part.

She spreads her arms out to be dramatic and leans forward and falls and falls and falls. Then, slowly, the wind shifts around her, twisted in invisible fingers, spins her, and spirals her up in a curve that shoots her back into the air, where she floats, legs bicycling, a giggle bubbling in her chest, before she arrow-darts forward, flying. And for the rest of the afternoon, she flies and flies and flies.

Something rings in her, and she stops, floating between canyon walls, and finds herself oriented eastward, and she knows, thousands of miles in front of her, at the end of her gaze, is a series of concrete buildings, a bundle of stone and metal and fluorescent light and blood and rust.

The first time she'd visited him, her brother had thought it was a dream. It'd been night after dinner and he'd been on the top bunk, unprotected from the too-bright light that buzzed loud enough to keep him awake, and he'd thought she was a hallucination, because what kind of person sees someone hovering at the end of their bed they haven't seen in half a decade? But he'd known not to speak, otherwise his cellmate woulda started bothering him, and he remembered that Ella could do things, strange things, things that ate up her insides, but she looked healthy, even with her hair completely gray. And without moving her lips, she told him that she was getting a handle on it, figuring out her gift, and Kev had stared at her in mute wonder as Ella played her adventures in his head. Ella saw him imagine her throwing an armored personnel carrier into a battalion of cops tricked out in riot gear. She sees him wondering if this knowledge would be enough to get the COs to stop hassling him, to get other guys in Gen Pop to stop fucking with him. Like people who fight ugly people who don't give a fuck about their face or how it'll end up and so got nothing to lose by going to the mattresses as hard as possible. They'll realize the girl who can throw an APC at a battalion of riot cops is his sister. That there's no conceivable reason for Kev to still be behind bars if he's got Ella on his team. And so it's madness that Kev's still here.

The first time she'd visited him, she'd seen that whole battle play across his face. You could get me out of here, but here is security and routine and a violence I already know too well. Then, at the end, a glimpse of old Kev as he throws a thought her way, more an aura of feeling and emotion and color than words. An admonition. Be careful, Ella. Don't let them know what you can do.

Unspoken between them, what they'd do to Ella if they ever found out what she was. And Ella wanting desperately to tell Kev that, in time, it won't matter. It won't matter what they could do to her, because they won't.

The light in his cell flickered, but by the time it came back on, she was gone. As Ella retreated to her New Haven apartment, she felt the aftermath of the visit hang like tendrils on her, the lingering navy-blue aura of grief, a tiny, whispering simulacrum of the feeling that had clung to Ella the first time she'd left them. When she'd seen fifty gunshots fired into Sean Bell's car, and, without warning, vanished.

"I don't want no ghost coming to see me," Kev had said without moving his mouth. "If I see you, I wanna see you for real."

"You ain't gonna ask who did this?" Kev doesn't need to point to the laceration at his temple and the bandage that struggles to cover the length of slice and can't.

Ella leans back in her chair across the table from Kev while loved ones or family or friends or old classmates or people settling a grudge or people burying a hatchet do this visit thing. She has her arms crossed, posture all defiant. Anger, unfamiliar and slow, swirls at the bottom of her gut, creeps into the back of her brain. "Nope," she says.

Kev leans forward and already has that conspiratorial convict hunch that cons have on TV or in movies. "You gonna read my mind or something? Scan one of the CO's brains or something? I bet you could just put your hand to the floor and get all the stories that ever passed through this place."

He's not wrong. Ella's mind had wandered into one of the female COs who stood by a wall with her baton cradled under her crossed arms. There's one inmate, a black guy with tight cornrows meeting with another dude, probably a brother or cousin who repped the same set, that she has made it her duty not to look at, and Ella knows, can probably tell without Diving, that they're fucking. Memories run like shards across her line of sight: the two of them on the outside, he with his crew when he was younger and she with her older cousin, both her and her cousin sporting big hoop earrings with their names in gold, walking back from the movies and passing the boy with his crew and the boy hollering at her and the big cousin telling the boy off in sharp, smooth, knife-blade Spanish. Then furtive sneaking from one's house or the other's to fuck after the girl'd gotten out of school, and the boy not doing well in class and his mother not around because she was working three jobs, and he couldn't bear to see an eviction notice slide under their door like it did to the people one floor up, so he starts slanging, and when he hollers at the girl with his new kicks and his chain (that will be snatched in a week or so and that he'll have to stomp someone out to get back), she smirks, and the cousin fights even harder to keep the girl away from that sweat-sheened, Carhartt-clothed, muscled, bejeweled embodiment of

Trouble. More fucking, then the girl goes to college, and the guy goes to jail for dope and a parole violation from a prior, and there's a guard shift and as he's lined up with the other inmates on his block, he looks out the corner of his eye and sees homegirl walking down the line tapping her baton against thighs he remembers she used to wrap around his back when they got the springs in her bedframe to squeak and groan.

"It wasn't her," Kev says, and Ella realizes she's been staring.

"I know." But Ella can barely concentrate because an inmate three tables ahead has a shank wrapped up and shoved into his rectum and Ella feels herself boofing. And in that inmate's mind's eye and now Ella's eye is an image, a flash, of tissue he stuck in the door's locking mechanism so that he could jiggle it open even though it showed up as closed on the guard's boards. Then a jagged, slow-motion clip of the inmate's plan to pop his cell after lights out and join two others who'd done the same to knife an Aryan whose son, on the outside, put that guy's son in the hospital at a Confederate flag rally.

"But that's the thing about the hospital, you know? You get your little bit of freedom. That's how you get it. That's how you get the attention you been dying to get. Gets to be a bit like home after a while."

"I ain't been around much." Ella dislikes that it feels

like an apology. She hasn't gotten to hate yet. "But you know how the fam is."

When Kev finally looks up from his folded hands, there's fear in his eyes. For the first time since Ella started visiting. In his brain are capsules, pills. Seroquel. Benadryl, drugs the medical staff give him, sometimes saved up so that he can just lie there and take a bunch at once and just wait for them to hit, only to wake up the next day and realize "Fuck, I can't do this." It's all in Kev's eyes, and Ella sees it, though her ephemeral fingers only touch the contours of that thought. And Kev asking her without opening his mouth: *you could burn it down; you could just burn this motherfucker down, all of it; please, just burn it down.*

She looks down, then up again and past her brother. There's an inmate talking to his baby's mother, and the inmate's leg is bobbing up and down because earlier in the day, he splashed a CO, threw urine all over the guy's face and soaked the front of his uniform, practically popped a balloon on him, then put his arms behind his head so that the cameras would see that he wasn't resisting or striking the CO. He knew that guy and a bunch of his buddies would be waiting for him, maybe right outside the showers in the cameras' blind spot, to put him in the hospital or maybe even kill him, and this might be the last time he sees his baby's face ever again.

The metal table dips where Ella's fingers press into it,

and she realizes what she's doing and takes her hand off and puts it in her lap.

An older man tells his grandson, brought in by his daughter, about how he's learning chess so that when he gets out he can play his grandson, who's getting really good, apparently. He says this, knowing he will not get out, that he will die either here or somewhere upstate where, he hears, the prisons are starting to turn more into hospices than anything else. But he still tells his grandson about how he's learning to play in solitary, because that makes his situation seem less scary, though his daughter knows exactly what a stay in the Bing entails. And the older man's words are brightly colored, even as Ella sees the man's imagination, sees the man and the inmate in the cell next door both drawing the board on pieces of paper and screaming their moves out to each other, and the loneliness washes purple over the image and reminds the older man about how dirty his cell was when he first moved in and how the only way to get Sanitation to come in and clean it was to stuff the toilet with books he was sent and flood the cell or to break the toilet so that the cell became unusable.

Ella wants to tell Kev to just survive, as though that would be enough. Just survive. But, in her chest, it becomes a cruel thing to ask him to do.

She doesn't want to reduce this entire compound—

its ten jail facilities with approximately sixty beds in each, its eight-by-ten solitary confinement chambers, its hallways and the cameras placed so that there were blind spots where the bleeding happened, and its railings and its bars and its slatted windows and its shitty air-conditioning—all to dust. She wants to be able to go port back in time, reach her hand in and put it to Kev's chest the night of that attempted armed robbery. Or to go back even further and stay closer to Kev for longer to keep him in that bubble of protection so that cops would leave him alone more often. Or to go back even further and keep him from becoming friends with Freddie, who would one day get picked up by cops for looking at one for too long and in the police van on the way to the station would get his spine severed. Because maybe if Kev didn't know him as a friend, as a brother, almost, in Ella's absence while Ella went to discover her powers where she couldn't hurt people, maybe Kev might not be here. Or maybe reach back even further and nudge Mama to bring the family somewhere else where the land didn't burn underneath them and catch fire, where they could settle and where white people were maybe a little less thirsty for his blood.

I'd stop time for you, Kev, she almost says.

The fear dampens in Kev's eyes, and Ella realizes Kev heard her anyway.

Brother and sister smile across the table at each other.

Later, as Ella gets up to leave and walks back to the gate, she brushes past a young woman and pain spikes through her spine, and she sees it: sees the Latina with the dark, wavy hair and the little Dominican boy at her knee and sees them at home and sees the Latina woman in the kitchen on the phone screaming upon hearing that her child's father has died and sees the Latina woman and the dead man's mother and their lawyer poring over the autopsy reports saying he'd had ulcers and reports and memos that indicated that, when they'd ruptured, the other prisoners had called for help while the guard on duty sipped coffee at his desk down the hall and watched. Ella sees the woman and her son return to the jail to pick up the decedent's things: a red Champ hoodie, his wallet, and a gray-red-and-black Bulls hat. The woman outside hugging herself against the cold and giving the sweater to her son, who is shivering.

———

Kev's in his cell the next time Ella sees him.

"Come with me," she says and takes his hand.

Night turns to day.

They don't know where they are, one of those parts of the country that's just open desert and brown-green shrub with mountains that are always far away and sky that is always blue, except when it's diamond-threaded black. They've Jumped. Kev's body is still in his cell. But with a single touch, Ella's hand on Kev's, his mind has been jettisoned elsewhere. She's been practicing.

"The South might as well be Chechnya to me," Kev says after he gets comfortable, and she wonders if he's thinking of another inmate, his cellie maybe, or someone he met who lingers in his memory.

They're leaning against motorbikes on a stretch of desert road, and Ella conjures a breeze and doesn't even need her hands to do it anymore. She's got them stuffed into the pockets of her ripped jeans, and all she needs is a cigarette for the picture to be perfect. Ella thinks of Malik and last night and how she discovered she could do this. On her mattress in the midst of an oppressively humid New York night, outlined in moonlight blue, they'd traveled at a stray thought from his twin mattress to a beach on the Dalmatian Coast. Feeling the mud of the shoreline in their toes, hearing the click of a woman's heels against the cobblestones, seeing the clearest, purest blue of the Mediterranean. Then they were back.

Ella looks at Kev, doesn't probe his mind, just looks at his face and the new grayness, the new hardness in it, the scars she can't see but feel. He doesn't look eighteen. If he thinks the South is like Chechnya, what does that make home?

Gray clouds circle far away and lightning forks down. A good two seconds later, they hear the boom.

The lightning strikes again, snaps at the earth with the recoil of a wet shower towel they used to whip each other with when they were just past being babies. Small fires puff to life.

Kev leans back against his bike and affects Ella's posture, and with them mirrored like that their minds bleed into each other and they trade images of apocalyptic landscapes south of the Mason-Dixon. Florida is riddled with radiation, ribbed by it, and craggy with decay. The Gulf of Mexico burps toxic waste onto the sores that litter Louisiana. Arkansas and Tennessee have turned blue and white under blankets of vengeful snow that come out of nowhere just to fuck with the climate change deniers. Then they get to Mississippi and Ella pauses because Mama sometimes talked about Mississippi and Ella imagines warmth and mosquitoes and tallgrass, haze more than smoke and lounging on cars with the smell of weed making a blanket and somebody's blasting Motown music out the open doors of their beat-up four-door and everybody is everybody's cousin and barbecue sauce is suddenly on people's fingers and bellies bulge with plenty. Maybe Mama didn't say all those things when she said the word "Mississippi." Maybe she didn't mention the mosquitoes or the music. But it was the only time Ella ever saw her not look like she was made of iron.

The fire spreads outward in a line, but never goes beyond the boundaries of the cloud cover, like it's trapped in a cylinder, and Ella thinks Kev's humming, but she can't tell 'cause of the wind. His eyes are closed, loosely. And he's feeling the air against his face, smiling while he does it. Then wind wraps its fingers around the fire and squeezes, and the cloud cover vanishes, too quickly.

"Wake up!"

The prison guard bangs his baton on the bars to Kev's cell, startling Ella and Kev out of the vision. Kev falls out of the dream and into his bed. Ella's afterimage hangs in the air. It takes all of her effort to keep from lashing out at the guard and decapitating him or stopping his heart or crushing his head. Her hand, translucent, comes up off of Kev's. Her astral projection lingers above his bed for only a moment before dissipating.

There are a million ways this can go, and Ella sees them all play out before her. In holographic projections that fill out and grow solid with wooden staircases that creak beneath boots and windows smudged so much you can barely see the rain or the snow or the sun outside, in the face that grows flesh and becomes warm to the touch, in the glint of sadness or joy or a mix of the two in the eyes.

She knew she would find herself back here. She didn't know whether she was going to port directly to the kitchen and wait or whether she was going to stand at the door like she does now. She didn't know if she was going to have to find another apartment or if what she was looking for would be in the same one she left all those years ago, but here it is, in front of her. The door, repaired and unmarked, like she had never lived in this place or walked up and down this stairwell when the elevator broke, lights flickering because the landlord will never repair the faulty electrical wiring.

She doesn't know what she will say. Whether she'll begin with an apology or whether she'll tell Mama that she has learned how to fly. But she knows that going to see Kev was preparation for this. For seeing Mama again.

In one version, she knocks, softly, and Mama opens the door, and surprise supernovas in Mama's eyes, and the two of them stand there, waiting for the worry that this is a dream to pass by, for the smoke to clear from the mirror. In another version, Mama guesses someone's presence at the door, and opens it to find Ella and looks at her as though she'd left just yesterday, like it was the natural order of the universe that brought her daughter back, like she knew Ella would do this all along. In another, the shock gives way to fear, and it shoots enough hurt into Ella's heart to remind her of what a bad idea this was and that she should never let Mama see her face again. In another version, Mama doesn't spend a single moment stunned. Her bottom lip trembles. Her eyes glass over with tears. She knows exactly what she's looking at, not a dream, not a nightmare wherein Ella stands before her one minute to be snatched away the next. She knows it's Ella she sees, and she's grateful, and she hugs Ella close to her chest, not forgetting that Ella could kill her with the wrong thought but trusting that she won't. That all the good things Ella will tell her about, all the ways she's brought her Thing under control, all the gifts she's been able to bring Kev with it, are true. And she'll sob tears of joy into Ella's shoulder, darken her shirt with gratitude, and whisper an urgent prayer of thanks that she passed whatever test God had put in front of her this time. With this, her gifted daughter.

Ella raises her fist to knock.

There's a bus called the Rikers bus.

Ella takes the M60-SBS from 125th Street. Usually she gets on at Lexington, sometimes before, depending on how late she was out the night before. Sometimes, after she moved to New Haven, she rises before the sun, beats it into New York, catching the beginnings of the sky's gilding just before the train glides over the bridge. The M60 takes her to Astoria Boulevard, where she transfers to the Q101 at 23rd Road. Sometimes schoolchildren ascend the steps and clog the main thoroughfare of the bus. Sometimes it's empty. Sometimes the only people on it other than Ella carry transparent plastic bags filled with the types of items permissible in the jail. And Ella knows exactly and immediately what they're going to be doing this morning. There's no camaraderie among the straphangers, no shared sense of enduring the city's indignities or of annoyance at the jail's security protocols or the idiosyncratic things that occasionally happen, like lockdown, when you're trapped in the jail and kept isolated from whatever horrible and hateful thing is being done to an inmate, maybe the very person you've come to visit. There's only a grim cloud hanging in the air between them, and they descend on Hazen and wait for the Q100, the Rikers bus, that will ferry them across the River Styx into the parallel, deathly reality that Rikers Island occupies. Where the circles of hell don't radiate outward but rather populate the space like satellite orbits.

She worries sometimes, whenever she gets onto the

Q101, that she's turning into one of the other women or the other men coming to visit friends, brothers, sisters, wives, husbands, fathers, mothers, guardians, godparents, bullies, victims, community pillars, the man who sold their mother crack. That deadness of the face. That unthinking that attends the packing of goods and materials to make sure no contraband is being brought into the jail facility.

When Kev and Ella sit in the visiting area, across the table from each other, Ella breathes a slow sigh. One time, they'd brought her to a different room where glass separated them and Kev had been escorted to his place in chains, having been dubbed that morning a problem inmate. There were no bruises on his face, yet, nor any discernible limp, but the shuffle very obviously masked some sort of hurt. Maybe his ribs.

This time, there are no chains. They let him walk freely, and his arms, though they don't swing far or wide, speak of that freedom.

He talks about parole, about watching guys get out, but doesn't sound too excited about it, because it'll be no different on the outside than on the inside and he's got some years before he's eligible. If he can stay out of trouble. No consorting with known felons; well, that means he can't even get a ride from Melo or Prodigy or anyone else on the block. Has to report regularly to his PO, and most POs are assholes and maybe this one won't even pick up his phone. Has to regularly report any change of address, etc., etc., etc.

Ella knows she should be excited for the possibility of him being let out, but she has Oscar Grant's murder in Oakland playing in her head and wonders if she would have the wherewithal to film Kev's death and upload it live. She doesn't know what she would do; maybe it is safer for Kev in here. And suddenly the thought of him on the outside, where so much has happened without him, terrifies her.

It's early in what's going to become a much longer stay than I ever expected. But I pick up things quick, have to, because I come in smaller than most of the others, and I start out in the juvenile ward, RNDC, before I get starred up and end up sharing a cell and a chow hall with the older niggas.

This old head named Ricky is standing over me taking hits from a Capri Sun in between bites from a chocolate chip cookie while I take my shit, and I got the palm of my hand against my eye to try and push back the headache that's making me go practically blind. I can't hear what Ricky's saying, only the mosquito-buzz of this nigga's incessant storytelling and supposed wisdom, and he says something about how jail sentences beget more jail sentences, and you're only supposed to be in Rikers for short sentences or pretrial and it's mostly niggas that can't afford bail here and something about making poverty illegal, and I wanna tell him to shut the fuck up with the voice I used to use in Harlem, the loud, commanding, brimming-with-violence voice. I have a different voice in here. I ask questions like "We have a problem?" or "Nigga, you good?" and I can mean "Do you need help?" or "You want me to fuck you up?" and it's like gang finger-shakes how people here immediately know the difference.

"Rick," I whisper. "Please, be quiet."

The headache lets up a little, but then I get dizzy, and I worry I'm gonna fall off this toilet with my jumpsuit around my ankles and my ass out in the air, and it's gonna be a wrap for me because Ricky here, or whoever, isn't gonna mind a little shit-dick. Ricky starts humming what sounds like an old Negro spiritual, a prison song, and I close my eyes tighter, and suddenly, I can feel Louisiana beneath me. A rush of color and sound and smell, then it's all gone. Headache and everything.

Whispers skip down the line of cells, and I finish my shit, wipe, and go to the bars to see niggas twisting their fingers and notes getting passed. Shit.

Under my bed are a bunch of *National Geographic* magazines. I pull them out with a roll of duct tape and start taping the issues around my torso. Ricky's got this sad look in his eyes, and I just tell him, without turning all the way around, "Stay in your cell for rec." And I see suddenly past his look and into the mess of feelings wrestling behind his eyes, his sorrow that this is now a Young Man's Game, that he has aged out of the everyday chaos of incarceration, gratefulness that this guy, Kev, NYSID Number 25768192Y, is looking out for him, wants to keep him safe, then the hard joy that comes with dodging the violence, a sort of glowing peace.

Out in the yard, we cluster. Eight by the pull-up bars, four on the basketball court, nine by the benches. One of the prisoners by the bench puts a leg up on the seat to mime tying his shoe and pulls out a homemade shank.

My group rushes them, and I feel nothing.

Rusty metal breaking jawline, fists smashing cheekbones and cracking ribs, someone getting a boot print stomped into their chest. It's gravity that smashes us together, and then we turn into electrons being flung apart by stuff larger than ourselves. It's all physics. The wild, swinging punches, the crumpling. The thwap of knuckles beating soft flesh, the dust rising to cover us, but unable to muffle the squawk of walkie-talkies and the foomp of the first gas canister being launched, and the coughing. The blood-rich coughing. All of this has the air of inevitability in it.

Burning takes my eyes and my face as I prowl for the rest of the fight, the tangle of bodies to get lost in. Someone's blood has already crusted on my knuckles.

"Get the fuck on the ground!"

I ignore the command, because that's how this is supposed to go.

The first volts seize through me, and I prepare to go down, but then I hear bones cracking. Through the smoke, the CO flying through the air to land on the ground somewhere in the distance. The earth rumbles beneath me, like it's getting ready to swallow me up. A crater forms. Then more and more craters form, and COs are shouting and screaming, then I hear the rubber bullets. More gas canisters. Then, eventually, darkness.

When I wake up, I'm naked in a single-man cell with a yellow piece of paper on my chest. There's a blue jumpsuit at the end of the green mat. The place still smells like the last three guys who got thrown here in AdSeg. Through the aching, I work my way into the jumpsuit, then, finally, pick up the paper to read it: "This prisoner is unmanageable in G.P. Loss of all privileges. No TV, no books, no sheets, no hygiene products, twenty-four-hour watch."

I'm in solitary.

I try to think about the last parts of the riot, the sound of the ground getting pushed in, breaking against itself, the CO flying through the air, arms swimming, before landing on his back and not getting up. If I can only regulate my breathing, I'll be all right. I just have to stay calm, but, because that's not how this is supposed to go, my headache is back.

My nose has been bleeding.

Ella has the rice and beans steaming in two plates, ready for Mama when she comes home from the hospital still in her scrubs. Mama never seems tired coming back from an overnight shift. She has never fallen asleep on the subway, stays alert all through the trek home, always takes the stairs, and keeps her eyes open all through the meal. And Ella wonders once again at her strength. She had tried once to massage calm and peace into her mother's mind, ease her into sleep, but Mama had shot back with a curt "Don't do that," before going to sleep on her own.

Mama takes her seat now in the kitchen and lets out a sigh. "Thank you for cleaning the bathroom."

Ella smiles. It's the least she can do, clean the place while Mama's at work, but Ella knows that Mama says these things because she knows Ella needs sometimes to feel useful. "You workin' again tonight?"

"Mmhmm," Mama says around a mouthful of beans.

"Do you wanna do something when you have a night off? See a movie or something?"

Mama looks up, then frowns. Silence stills the air between them. Mama puts down her fork. "What's in those boxes, Ella?"

Ella looks behind her, feigning surprise, at the shoeboxes. When she turns back, she can't look Mama in the face. "I just thought, you know, if you needed the money—"

"Where'd that money come from?"

Ella wants to snap at her, bark that she has a Thing that nobody else has, a gift that she can use and that all her life, she's been giving and giving and giving and now why not take something somebody's not gonna miss and it's not like she took it all from one person or even like she's robbing anyone they know. Ella wants to spit the words out, that she's tired of skimming, of snatching food from supermarkets or making toilet paper vanish off bodega shelves. She can destroy an entire building, she can plumb the depths of any person's mind and find their worries and their wants and she can twist them. She can make things fly. "Why don't you want it?" It comes out as a hiss.

"I don't need it."

"Yes, you do."

"Ella, I don't need this." She's standing now, palms heavy on the table, arms shivering with the weight.

"Mama," she growls. And in her mind, scenes replay. The chaos of the trauma ward, blood-slick tile floors that oiled gurney wheels squeak over, commands issued over the body of a man bleeding out from his gunshot wounds, Mama at the trauma surgeon's side as the team opens up the patient's abdomen, the gape the size of a basketball, Mama later sopping up the stomach acid leaking from the exposed intestines with gauze, then hooking the man up to a machine that sucks the acid out; Mama opening the door to another patient's room to see two hulking men in T-shirts and shorts looming over the bed, Mama thinking they're family. Then the men jumping back and telling her they're plainclothes cops and this patient's the suspected shooter. Mama wishing they'd leave the boy alone for just a little bit, not interrogate him and get ready to lock him up while the vertical incision from just below his nipple to his belly button was still fresh, while the kid was still reeling with just having had his kidneys removed and his spleen and part of his stomach, while the kid lies there as raw and open as the wound they can't yet stitch back together. And how could Mama not want to leave all that behind?

"It's wrong, Ella. And I don't need wrong in this house."

"You could buy a new one."

Ella stands, snatches her jacket off the back of her chair, and leaves without another word. Outside, she lets visions wash over her. Of Mama attending to a little black boy shot in the arm, Mama assisting the surgeon as the surgeon massages the heart back to life. Then that same little black boy, not even six months older, back with a gunshot wound to his upper arm, his brachial artery almost bleeding out, almost dying again, then the boy before Mama's eyes for a third time, shot in the head. Dead.

She's halfway up the block to a nearby park when she stops. She can't let herself get this angry. Not again. A couple deep breaths later, she heads back and is at the door again, but it opens without her key. Which means Mama never locked it.

"Mama?" Her "I'm sorry" dies on her lips.

Mama lies on the floor, her legs tangled beneath her, her arms splayed out, limp. Urgency radiates from her body. Even before Ella rushes to her side and fumblingly checks to see if she's breathing and thanks God that she is and calls for an ambulance and helps them get Mama into the back without even bothering to hide the shoe boxes, crumpled and conspicuous, in their kitchen, even before getting to the hospital where she'll watch over Mama as she recovers from what she'll tell Ella was "just a fall," Ella knows that as long as Mama's alive, she can't ever let herself get that angry again.

"I'm not leaving," she says at Mama's bedside. "Mama, I'm not leaving."

Eyes closed, Mama squeezes Ella's hand. Ella knows she should be thankful, but she can't get herself all the way there, because she knows the only reason Mama's squeezing her hand is because she knows Ella needs sometimes to feel useful.

"Have you ever been to a rodeo?" Kev asks. There's quiet eagerness in his voice the next visit, a thin, fast-moving river. "You know. Horses, bulls?"

"No," Ella manages behind her smirk. It's good to

see Kev animated like this. For a time, after his stint in solitary, he didn't say much. Some visits, he said nothing, and it was always a tiny miracle that he took her visits to begin with. He could just as easily have refused. Or been denied.

"They had rodeos at the prison where I was held before they transferred me up here." As he speaks, he does not look at Ella; he seems to look everywhere else, at the COs who walk alone or in pairs throughout the visiting room or along the hallways seen through the smudged glass of the entrance and exit doors or at the dust motes that, to Ella, would occasionally swirl to mimic the features of someone's face, a loved one's, an enemy's, a passing stranger's. "You know how it is down there. They couldn't do it to slaves anymore, so they put collars around our necks and did it to us. Field niggas. Just hoein' away. Pretty much picking cotton." At her knee. "The sheriffs sit on horses with their shotguns at their shoulder." At the floor. "The Passage." Out the window. "And you got a lotta niggas locked up for petty shit. Larceny, that sort of thing. Property crimes." At her. "They called it Angola. In case you forgot it all comes back to Africa." Which makes Ella breathe a nervous chuckle.

Underneath the table, Kev shifts one of his pant legs up, touches the skin of his ankle to the skin of Ella's.

Ella does not have to close her eyes to see what Kev sees; the vision, the memories, the past as he remembers it, all of it bleeds slowly then with increasing volume into Ella's brain, as though a cord were connecting his mind to hers. It begins with sights: children dressed in Polo shirts and jeans and dresses with golden and brown and black hair, smiling or frowning or laughing with their blue, green, brown, black, morning-colored eyes in the front row of the stadium; the striped prison uniform; the black and white of one prisoner's shirt as he stoops down, nappy hair shorn close to his skull, and pulls out a handful of identical shirts, stripes spraying in all directions, patterning him and the ground around him; other prisoners, elderly ones aged too quickly by what prison does to a person, their striped shirts tucked into stone-washed blue jeans, which are, in turn, tucked into knee-high leather boots. Then the sounds: the shimmering of a melody from the merry-go-round on the prison grounds, the hum of chatter between the incarcerated selling wares they had crafted in their workshops, magical and shining things, and the free folk who hold up those glimmering belt buckles to the light or who turn over the intricately detailed wood carvings in their fingers or who marvel at the necklace of beads held together by near-invisible thread, the creaking of a metal fence on which leans the chest of an inmate, her arms and tattooed hands dangling over, one of them bandaged and wrapped in gauze up past the wrist. Then the smells: the bull shit in the holding pens, the sweat-stink of prisoners unable to ask the air to press moisture into the skin, God unwilling to answer that prayer, sitting or standing motionless in their cages in the thick wool of their striped gowns and striped shirts; the perfume wafting off the girl whose long blond hair comes down in smooth threads to the small of her back, her face shaded by a large black cowboy hat, a black button-down shirt clinging to a shapely frame, tucked into tight jeans that raise her ass as she walks. Miss Rodeo Louisiana, making the rounds, waving to the families in the stands, waltzing past the cages that hold prisoners rendered hideous by the climate and their captivity.

"They had us stand in a circle in the middle of the ring," Kev says. "Only the well-behaved got to do this part. We got to wear special rodeo outfits, the white shirts with the blue triangles on the shoulders and every-thing, tassels, glitter, all of it. We held hands around four prisoners who held up flags, America's, Louisiana's state flag, a Confederate flag, and one other one I never figured out, Aryan Nation or something. And one of us sang the National Anthem over the speakers, then afterward, we bowed our heads and a minister came and said a prayer over the loudspeakers. Everyone had their eyes closed and their heads bowed, everyone in the stands."

The described world overwhelms Ella, all of its texture and scent and color invading her through her own empathetic touch, funneling into that space between her ears. She can see it all. She can feel, smell, taste, hear it all: four inmates, two of them with their silver hair in rattails, one of them with nappy hair and octogenarian eyes, one of them barely having finished being a child, their feet digging into the dirt, their legs bent slightly at the knees, hands open, fingers flexing, in a posture of readiness, attack, defense, toes light against the inner rims of the pink hula hoops at their feet. The gate clangs open and thundering toward them is the bull, eyes trained on the small coterie of collared prisoners, horns lowered, legs pumping, muscles rippling, dirt flecking its flanks, its hooves thudding against recently turned dirt and the compacted subsoil beneath. It flicks its head and one of the prisoners sails through the air, legs spread, a new gash torn through the side of his safety vest, his pain having pushed his face past contortion into an aspect of peace before he slams against the ground, body cracking in a way only he and the prisoners in the ring and Ella, who is there too, can hear.

One of the others darts from the path of the bull while another manages to step aside with one foot, the other firmly planted, his whole bearing intent on winning, even as the bull's skull crashes into another inmate. This one's unable to breathe through newly broken ribs, grips the bull's horns as tightly as can be managed, the bull throwing its head back and forth until the inmate's grip slips. The bull rushes over him, crushing a leg and an arm before cruising toward that last prisoner. He sees he's won the game of inmate pinball, runs for the edge of the ring and vaults to the top of the wall, just as the bull's horns bong against the metal reinforcing the cushioned plastic.

Kev's eyes are hot and glowing when Ella sees him again, across that table in the waiting room. He's sweating, breathing heavily, smiling. Anguish pulls Ella's heart into the floor. This is the other side of what solitary did to him. The agitation, the running straight into painful memories rather than barricading himself against them. Whatever destructive impulses propelled Kev that night of the attempted armed robbery now augmented by what twenty-three hours in a cell alone for six months will do to a man. Kev looks as though he is staring at the sun, intent on blindness.

Ella manages to make it onto the Rikers bus heading back into Queens before crying. Her heart shakes in her chest. Kev has never been to the Louisiana State Penitentiary.

———

She moves the blinds by the kitchen window and watches the police patrol the block. Up and down St. Nicholas, they amble. Stationed on one corner, an officer sits in his mini-tank and says something that the cop walking by laughs at. The guns on the small tank's turret are angled toward the ground. Metal orbs float along the sidewalks above the streetlamps, close enough for people to see, not bothering to disguise themselves, but everyone has already gotten used to them. They've quieted the neighborhood. The park across the way holds only the rustling of empty burger wrappers and soda cups. Her hands are shaking against the window blinds, and she feels it coming. Small pulses matching her heartbeat that radiate out of her to rattle the cutlery and unsettle the grill on the stove. They'll see her.

The smell of sulfur swallows her.

Her eyes burn and when she opens them again, above her, a gray sheet for sky, and before her, a sign showing she has arrived at Belmont Park in Elmont, New York, outside of the outside of the City, where there are houses and strip malls, where cars have space to breathe on the boulevards. On the jumbotrons in the main building, white college students in loafers, seersucker suits, and their dates in broad hats, watch the Kentucky Derby alongside bomber-jacketed South Asians.

Ella wanders to the clubhouse. Nobody turns her way. She's Shielded.

The tents and the front terrace are spotted with families and bearded, potbellied middle-aged white men tipping back cans of Bud Light. The kids, baby-faced and gleefully, obnoxiously tipsy, must be from St. John's, prancing as they do now like the horses about to race, while the girls, in their gowns and gaudy, wide-brimmed hats, pull beer coolers behind them like servants. Bow ties clinch necks, sleeves rolled up, sunglasses worn indoors.

In clusters, at various points in the clubhouse, like scattered molecules, close to the exit onto the track and below the grandstand, wait people who look like they're from around here. Familiars. The thick two-hundred-page paper programs of the day's races rolled up in their nicotine-stained fingers. Weathered jackets and sweats and jeans loose on them, some of them with shirts tucked into their pants, they all crane their necks in anxious penitence, some of them marking their programs absently, others clutching their betting slips. Weathered white faces, all of them. No fear of gun turrets or constant ob-

RIOT BABY

servation. This place doesn't need to be watched. A burst
of anger flames in her heart, a small one, swallowed up
a moment later by pity. Wasting away, and if they saw
Ella, they'd still think they were inherently better.

Everywhere has a patina of dirt and dark, even
though the sun has finally beaten back the cloud cover
outside. A few patrons light up cigarettes as they brush
past her, still unaware of her presence. Ella shuffles to
a booth, reaches over a counter, feet dangling off the
ground, then comes back up with a beer.

A heavy-set man nearby in glasses and a goatee
speaks urgently into a flip phone: "I'm tellin' you; she
can't keep doing this. Every month she's in jail. Every
two weeks." He drifts out of earshot.

Someone behind her shouts an epithet.

Even here, the inevitable violence.

Ella, a few gulps into her beer, goes back and makes
herself a Bloody Mary. The ingredients pour themselves
out of their bottles. The stirrer shimmies its way out of
its plastic box container and dances inside the glass. A
brief promenade out to the track and she sees more of
the bedraggled track-dwellers. A few of them congregate
around a bench and chat, catch up, wonder out loud
about the tactile realities of their world. The game, the
kids, the front lawn. Many of them don't pay attention to the races, the track often unoccupied for long

stretches of time. There are some kids in leather jackets and fitted caps playing reckless games of tag, hopping over the metal benches and their dividers. Other white kids either pick at their fathers' collars when they're being carried or crush empty beer cans beneath their feet.

How much of that little girl's lunch money for the year had been put on a horse that will run in a few hours?

If you had an addiction, Ella says to the Kev in her thoughts, you wouldn't let your kids get in the way.

Back on the terrace, Ella steals a program and, perched over a small table in the front courtyard, scans for the next race.

The program lists, for her race, seventeen horses, and Ella smirks when she sees their names. Morning Glory, Valley of Lillies, O'Doul's Revenge, Corp d'Esprit, and on it goes, random phrases purloined from a number of languages, meaning nothing except what significance the phrase held for the horse's wrinkled white owner. Ella had seen some of the horses out front on the track while another made a lazy trot around, its jockey swaying in the saddle. Testing the hooves maybe or engaged in some other esoteric ritual Ella can't begin to understand.

These outings fill her with a gleeful cruelty. She'd walked around these white people invisible, on the racetrack, in the trailer park villages, outside the pubs, and seen nothing but squalor and waste. In some places, hypodermic needles litter the floor and babies, when they cry, reveal teeth rotted by the Mountain Dew that's cheaper than the milk their mothers want to buy. She wants to show this to Kev. See how little they are, brother. Knowing that jail tries to tell someone that all their betters are on the outside. They're not better than you out here, Kev. None of them are.

In the larger building, Ella lowers her shield to bet on an Irish horse to place and a French horse to win. If Kev were here, she'd tell him, "Logic says, you can win big but you can only lose small." And Kev would take maybe two and a half seconds before pointing out the holes in her proof, the missteps. But you don't go to a racetrack to win money, these white people have taught her. You go to lose money. And what did it matter? she would ask him. She'd get their money to magically reappear, stolen from someone else's pocket, or maybe pulled from thin air with her Thing.

The French horse has the longest odds. But Ella doesn't care, not yet. Her gray horse—already "hers"—puts in a stronger-than-expected showing, but finishes middle of the pack, not even enough to show, though she had bet on it to win. Ella approaches the betting machines and gives them more money, punches keys and presses buttons according to the day's philosophy, which has been, and remains, that if you bet long you can only lose what you put in, and if you bet long, you could win so much more than that.

Ella found the first race more amusing than thrilling, but it has gotten her going, and she watches the next Derby race and the next Belmont race, both close, on screen. She'd chosen her Derby horse quickly. In a race with seventeen horses, there was no hope. The next Belmont race promises more. Ella vacillates between Number 1 and Number 3. Number 1 has 10–1 odds, and Number 3 starts out 6–1.

Trackside, she fishes a coin out of her pocket. For an instant, the sun peeks through the cloud cover to glint on the thing. Her smile has wickedness in it. She flips the coin, and it stays in the air longer than coins normally do. It lands in her palm, and she slaps it onto the back of her free hand. Number 1 it is.

She flips it again, not playing with it this time. Horse Number 1 again.

She returns to the machine and bets on Horse Number 3.

The race begins. All around her, faces spasm in ecstasy and panic. Fists pump, betting slips crinkle, backs seize, shoulders tense. Feet tap. Stomp. Knees jitter. When the race finishes, an obnoxious bow-tied frat boy runs to a white girl in a hoodie and shouts, "We just won one million dollars!" on a 5–2 horse.

"Fuck that guy," Ella mutters.

Then she hears a ghost of Kev whisper in her ear, "To win a million on a 5–2 horse, you have to already bet more than you should have. They didn't make that much," he says, smirking like he's seen this many times before.

How often now had she come to watch white misery and provincial white joy? She has the ease of someone who has walked through sewer water before, knows to take off her shoes and socks and roll up her pant legs, knows the routine of watching for detritus, for broken glass. How much time has she spent watching these people? With them but not of them? She feels suddenly assured. This is what I did when I vanished, she hopes she can eventually tell Kev. Show him.

Around her, people split $10 and $5 bets on a few horses, one to win and maybe a few others to show or place. The seasoned ones mark up their programs and have pockets stuffed with tickets that will later litter the floor in pieces.

The next Belmont race starts off and Number 3, around the halfway mark, slips back. Number 1 breaks ahead, snaps the tape by a sizable length, and Ella watches it gallop away with the $260 she would've won if she'd listened to that damn coin.

The sky has started to darken.

Back at her kitchen table with its view of the surveillance tower at the top of the hill and the mini-tank at the corner of 145th and St. Nicholas and the mechanized orbs doing their controlled flight over Sugar Hill, night has fallen.

———

Ella has seen nothing but hospital rooms. At Mama's bedside, her hand on Mama's while Mama sleeps, swimming deeper and deeper into Mama's mind, then letting the current pull her wherever it wishes, she sees nothing but hospital rooms.

A sound. A beep. When Ella looks up, Mama's on a table in a small, dark room with a monitor hooked to her, her swollen belly wet with gel, her face turned to the monitor where she watches the heartbeat beep and beep. Ella follows her gaze, watches the green lines trace mountain peaks and valleys, then slowly turn to chicken scratching. In the ultrasound, the grainy image of a fetus moves, then stops. A nurse leaves the room, but there's someone else there, dressed in a multicolored gown with beads around her neck and wrists. She holds a bag, and the odor of lavender wafts luxuriously from it. The two of them, Mama and the black lady, stare at each other, and Ella watches the black lady smile reassurance into a Mama who looks younger than Ella ever remembers her being.

"I'm anxious," Mama says. "But I'm ready."

"You're ready," the lady says back. She reaches into her sack and pulls out papers covered in crayon scribblings. Affirmations like "I can do this" and "I am loved" and "I am strong."

The doctor returns and says to the room, "We don't want to wait. We're going to get her out now." And Ella follows the nurse and her mother and this other woman up several flights of stairs to the labor and delivery unit, and the woman changes into purple scrubs, her sack now filled with snacks she got from the vending machine on the ground floor.

Ella stands by the wall as the doctor, brisk and white, enters with a clipboard in his hands. "Have you had any children before?" the doctor asks without looking up.

The woman frowns. "Have you even read her file?" And the two of them glare at each other for a moment.

"A stillborn," Mama says, and the air vanishes from Ella's lungs. This is new. She has never been here before. She'd walked through so many of Mama's memories that she could describe them down to the chipping on the walls: Mama leaving abusive partners, Mama at church, Mama at the club with girlfriends, Mama praying by her bed at their home in South Central, Mama as a kid running through Mississippi backyards. How deep Ella must have gone to get here. But she doesn't try to leave, doesn't try to force herself out of the memory. The current brought her here. Mama brought her here.

"The demise was last year?"

Mama stiffens at the word.

The woman touches the doctor's arm and says, "May I speak to you outside?"

After a moment, Ella follows them, passing through the door as though it were a curtain, and she watches the woman tell the doctor to please make a note in Mama's chart about the stillbirth, how every time she has to recite her trauma, Mama's mind goes back to that place of anxiety and fear and heartbreak.

"She's having a high-risk delivery," the woman says. "I would hope that her care team would thoroughly review her chart before walking into her room."

For a moment, the doctor is silent. Then he says, "You doulas shouldn't even be here. You're lucky I don't call security."

Ella follows the doula back into Mama's room, and

it's as though time stretches like a rubber band before snapping in place, because now there are tired lines on Mama's face and she groans like she hasn't had a drop of water in hours.

"Can I get an epidural?" Mama murmurs to the anesthesiologist nearby, who shoots the doula a look that gets the doula out of the room.

Ella stays, then watches the white woman administer a spinal dose of anesthesia. Ella's fists tighten at her sides when she watches her mother clench her own fists and grit her teeth. When the doula returns, Mama's head shoots up from her pillow, and there's rage in her eyes.

"I can't feel my legs," she hisses. Then her head falls back. "And my head." That last comes out as a moan.

"What did you give her?" the doula asks the anesthesiologist.

Mama's blood pressure rises. Ella can feel it like heat rising in her own face. She looks at the numbers on the screen, another heart rate, the baby's heart rate. It's dropping.

The doula crouches at Mama's side and grips her hand in both of hers. "What happened was wrong," she says in a whisper, "but for the sake of the baby, it's time to let it go."

Mama grits her teeth. She's not ready to let it go.

"Close your eyes," the doula tells her in the softest voice Ella has ever heard. "What's the color of your stress?"

"Red."

"What color relaxes you?"

Mama takes several mountainous breaths. "Lavender."

The beeping stabilizes. Mama's blood pressure drops. Ella's fists unclench.

A team of three young female residents hurry into the room with the delivery nurse behind them, a flurry of white, then a man who looks like the attending physician, and he introduces himself briefly before plunging his hands between Mama's legs, and the question shines bright in Mama's eyes, through reflexive tears, and the doula sees it and says, "What happened to Dr. Rosenbaum? He was supposed to be here." But the doctor doesn't explain the switch, instead pulling his hands out and snapping off his gloves and saying, "She's ready. Time to push."

And they all get to work, a small hurricane of white while the doula, the only other black woman in the room, leans by Mama's side and says, "You're a rock star. You can do it. This is it. You can do it. You're doing amazing. Push! You can do it!"

And Mama pushes and pushes, not taking her eyes off the doula. And Ella watches her own head appear, a slick cluster of black curls. And Mama pushes again, and the young resident takes baby Ella's head and eases the slippery body out, and the residents all take turns between Mama's legs, but when Ella looks up, the attending physician is gone, almost like he wasn't here, and it's only the young white women and the doula and Mama sobbing shaking laughing as she watches her baby girl, purple and wrinkled and stone-still, touch air for the first time.

A resident lays the baby on Mama's chest. "Is she all right? She's not moving. Is she okay?" Then, a second later, the baby's tiny arms and legs tense, and she opens her mouth and lets out a cry.

"She's perfect," the doula tells Mama.

"I did it," Mama breathes. "Oh, Ella," she says, looking to the baby, as she touches a back slick with blood and amniotic fluid. "I did it."

Ella blinks, and the room is empty. The residents have vanished. So has the doula. So has the baby.

Mama is older. She's back to now.

Mama's eyes flutter open. "Baby, why you crying?"

Ella dashes away the tears. She blubbers an apology.

"Oh, baby. It's going to be all right."

"I almost killed you."

Mama puts her hand over Ella's. "Baby, you ain't never do no such thing."

A few moments later, Ella calms her sobs enough to ask, "How come you never told me about . . . about the stillbirth?"

Pain glints in Mama's eyes, but it's gone the next instant. "That was a long time ago. And—" Headaches and light sensitivity bleed from Mama, through their intertwined hands, into Ella. She sees the argument with the boyfriend and him grabbing the knife and her screaming, "Back up! I have a baby," and the police arriving. Feels the swollen hands and feet and face and the doctors telling her just to take some Tylenol, always more Tylenol, then the day before the baby shower when her aches had become too much and a doctor scribbling 143/86 in a chart during her appointment. And her doctor telling her to lie down then telling her that he was going on vacation and she could deliver the baby by C-section that day if she wanted, six weeks early, then the car ride a few days later on the way to her boyfriend's and the wetness between her legs which is not water like she expects but blood. In the rush afterward, someone saying that elevated blood pressure had separated her placenta from her uterine wall, then haziness and Mama asking over and over again, "Is he all right? Is he all right?" Then the silence of the delivery room. The most deafening silence Ella has ever heard in her life.

It's gone the next instant.

"It was so long ago," Mama whispers. "I'd hoped to keep that from you."

"But why, Mama?"

Mama looks to the ceiling. "You're always so angry. I . . . I didn't wanna add to your burden."

"Just like you weren't gonna tell me about your cancer?"

Mama flinches. Just enough for Ella to notice. "I don't wanna fight it. I just—" Then she allows herself a moment of release, of bitterness. "These doctors ain't gonna help me with that anyway." Then she's back. She pats Ella's hand. "It's just enough that you're here."

When Mama slips back into slumber, Ella slides her hand out from beneath her mother's. It's not until she exits the hospital, leaving behind a double to watch for any change in condition, that she realizes the gift Mama has just given her.

Mama had seen the look in Ella's eyes when Ella had said "I almost killed you," then she had let Ella see what she saw.

"*They* almost killed you."

Mama's only moment of bitterness. Of rage, of

malice, of hurt. The only moment of truth into which she had let her daughter.

And it's enough to set Ella free.

———

They don't tell me why I finally got out of solitary, but I'm pretty sure it's because there's not enough space in the jail, and I gotta make room for another guy.

Routine snaps back with a quickness. There's the heart attack or the epileptic fit, then suddenly, the body reasserts itself and starts working again. A little different than before, maybe a little slower. Maybe it has to engineer a few workarounds, but soon enough, I'm in a cell, and I got a cellmate, and I have a new job fixing computers for a local public school, because someone finally explained to a CO who told Administration why some of the inmates call me Techie.

The block gets called to breakfast at 7 a.m., and by 7:30, I'm working. But, today, unease gets my fingers twitching. Another heart attack's coming. It's late: 6:20, and the cell lock still hasn't disengaged. I get up and look out down the walkway to see everyone else still locked in their cells.

"Deuce," I say to the big guy still sleeping in his bed. "Deuce, the ninjas are coming."

He slaps his gums. "Wake me up when they get here," he says, then rolls all 275 pounds of his body over.

The tablet I usually use to scroll through and read up on what news comes through the few websites we get access to is propped up by the toilet, where I usually take care of another part of my morning routine, the privacy sheet taped up to one end so that it hangs diagonally over the halfway mark of our cell.

We don't have much by contraband, but I make a mental note, just so we have something to give the COs when they come through. If the cell's clean, they'll stick around for too long, expecting to find real dirt. Give them a little of what they're looking for, and they'll stop looking, Terrell had told me once after I'd starred up and got moved out of RNDC.

The tablet. Shit. Thumper's tablet. They find that and I'm back in AdSeg, then waiting for me when I get back out will be no job, no privileges, and no Deuce, who might be one of the only guys in here with a routine that doesn't fuck with mine.

"Deuce, the fucking tablet."

He's up on the edge of his bed now and yawns. "Fuck it. Can't do nothin' 'bout it now, nigga."

In the middle of the block, the support team is already setting up a table for paperwork. Empty boxes surround it.

Two-man teams go into each cell. A little Roomba goes in with them, sometimes before, to scan first for anything that might get them or anything they might miss. There's been talk that these guys are Augments, wired up like comic book superheroes. An inmate's entire history gets beamed into their system, so they know if you're trouble, they can tell what privileges you've been granted, who's ever visited you and what they might've smuggled to you. They know what you've boofed without having you strip and spread your cheeks. There's no hiding from these niggas.

They're getting closer. Cellies get out and get cuffed, then stand by and watch as their cell gets tossed. Papers, nudes taped to the wall, extra sheets, stuff out of commissary.

Deuce has already started stripping his bed, and I start on mine. We fold our sheets and blankets, unplug our fans and wrap up the cords. Deuce leaves a few of his issues of *Hustler* around in strategic locations so they'll get found.

Then the beep as they reach our cell.

I try to get a read on them as Deuce and I walk out and get cuffed and the Roomba goes in. They look bored more than anything else, but even the bored niggas can decide to make an example out of you for no reason in particular and "search" your shit by dumping coffee all over your papers, then walking all over them. And even the bored guys might see the tablet on its stand there, looking at them like a middle finger, and strike us.

I'm dizzy with worry, waiting for a head to poke out.

Then, after what seems like an hour, the Roomba crawls out, and the two guys follow and uncuff us and let us back in. It's still there.

Almost like someone had put a blanket over it. Shielded it.

The inmate-porters sweep up the mess and push the contraband left over closer to the cells so inmates can put a hook on a string, toss it under our doors, and pull back our shit.

They let us out into the yard later the next day, and I spot Terrell across the way, but before I can say what's up, I hear the smack of knuckles against cheek and already a crowd has gathered around the fight breaking out.

I feel my hands ball into fists. I don't know either of the cats duking it out, not the big guy, not the little nigga, but the fire warms in me nonetheless until a CO shouts, "All right, guys. Knock it off."

A couple dozen guards fill the yard, but nobody moves, except for a few that have their pepper spray and their shock-sticks turned on.

The CO who called out earlier does it again, half-heartedly, bored. Four more guards come out, and the first guard, now with backup, gets closer just as the big guy goes down. The guards beat the smaller guy with their shock-sticks just as the big guy drops the shank he was holding.

I don't know what it is about today, but I feel protected. Maybe it's the tablet.

The fight cuts our rec time short, and pretty soon, we're back in the hall, two officers behind us, one for each line we've formed, holding their shock-sticks.

We're coming down a flight of stairs when one of the COs, a younger guy I don't recognize, stops next to me and nods for me to go back up. The others stop at the bottom of the stairs. Everyone's looking, and I see in their eyes the look of brothers making sure nothing evil gets done to their family. There's a chaplain waiting for me at the top of the stairs.

"You have to call home," he says, in a voice too kind for this place.

From the kitchen window, Ella can just barely catch the edge of the Baptist church two blocks down. They'd had immigrant neighbors above them when they lived in that apartment, and one day, Mama had started praying differently. She would pray like they did, like every step on

American soil was sacrosanct. The type of prayer that enlisted her whole body. Ella remembers peeking at Mama when she was supposed to have closed her eyes and how it felt like she was looking at a superhero bathed in the light of the sun from which she'd gained her powers. It was how she'd prayed right before Kev caught that attempted armed robbery charge. It was how she'd prayed after Ella's self-exile. And whenever Ella would return to the changing neighborhood and spy on Mama, she'd see that it was how she'd prayed after that white kid in Charleston, South Carolina, had walked through the doors of that church, joined a Bible study group just like Mama's, and then pulled out a .45-caliber pistol before opening fire.

Ella hated that kind of prayer. Sounding like they should be grateful just to be here. She remembers reading about that kid who killed those churchgoers, and she remembers praying for revenge. Praying for frogs and locusts and for rivers of blood, for every Confederate flag to find its own funeral pyre.

She'd cried a lot back then.

The videos had been ubiquitous, some more explicit than others. Six shots into the back of a man fleeing arrest on a child support warrant, or two shots ringing out and cops standing over the prone bleeding body of a young man in the midst of protests commemorating the anniversary of another boy killed by a cop. After each one, Ella had Traveled. Straight to the site of the killing, and she'd touched the ground, breathed in the air, and sucked that history deep into her body. Inhaled the violence of the previous hours. Sometimes it felt pornographic. To go to that cul de sac in McKinley, Texas, where black kids younger than her sat on the ground, handcuffed, while their white neighbors jeered and one cop grabbed a girl in a bathing suit by the arm and hurled her to the ground, then dug his knee into her back while she wailed for her mother.

She'd returned from every trip with her head in her hands.

What if I'm the answer? she had asked herself. What if I'm the one we've been praying for?

Two blocks away, in an apartment across the street from the Baptist church, a phone rings.

———

There's no one in the sergeant's office when we get to it. The chaplain waits in the doorway and I want to smack that pitying look off his face, but then the door closes. I wait for someone to come in and tell me what to do or to hold out a phone for me to answer into, but nobody comes. I go to the phone on the wall, pick it up, and dial. It rings three times before something cold washes over me, and when I turn back to the desk, Ella's holding herself, like she's trying to keep from being torn apart.

I drop the phone.

"Ella, what . . . what are you doing here?"

"Nobody can hear us," she says. Her doing. Her Thing.

This is it. The reason nervousness had spider-walked along my spine this morning. I steel myself. "Yeah?"

"Mama's gone."

My jaw twitches, and I fight to stand still. But my hands, my legs, my whole body is trembling. People don't live forever. People die every day. Some of them die unlucky, they all die either way. And there's no order to it, it happens to all of us, but this. Ella said they couldn't hear us, but I know if I let go, they'll hear me wail. They'll have an idea what it's about, and maybe some of them would understand, but they'll hear it anyway, and I can't let them hear it.

I close my eyes against the scream building in my throat. My whole body tenses. The ground shifts beneath me. Books shuffle along the shelf and nearly fall off. The paperweight on the sergeant's desk dances to the edge. Chairs scrape along the floor.

"Kev."

Someone's calling my name, but all I see is black. All I hear is the roar in my ears.

"Kev."

Tear this place down.

"Kev."

I want to see her. I want to see her so bad, and maybe if this place is erased, maybe that'll bring me closer. The dust in the air stills. Electricity sparks to life around me. I can hear it pop.

"Kev!"

Then it's gone, and I'm cold again.

For a long time, we stare at each other.

"Aight, then," I say. That's it. I feel like it's over, even though I have no idea what "it" is. Either way, something important is finished. Ain't no reason to be here anymore. Ella takes a step closer, and I know she means to hug me, but I put an arm out to stop her. "You ain't gotta do that. You're a ghost too."

I don't wait for her to vanish before I open the door and walk back out into the hall.

"Take a walk, Deuce," I tell him when I get back.

He peers up over the top of the *Hustler* he was thumbing through and looks me over, and I know he's doing the calculations in his head, knows the news I got is the person-shattering kind and sees it, even though my words came out calm and measured. And he knows what I'm gonna do because he's seen it before or, like all of us, has heard of it happening, and on the outside, maybe he would've tried to stop it, but because this is what happens in a place like Rikers, he merely folds his magazine back up, stuffs it under his mattress, and walks to the cell door, leans on a bar with his arms out and makes to start conversation with a neighbor.

My body moves like a machine. I take my sheet and tear it and, even though I've never done this before, I know just how to tie the knot and just how to get the sheet over the bar from which our privacy sheet hangs. I know how to test its strength without yanking the bar out, and I know how to make sure it's all set up high enough that when I step off my bed, my feet won't touch the floor.

In less than a minute, it's all set up.

I'm up and have the makeshift noose around my neck, and I'm about to step into my blank future when I smell sulfur.

When I look up, I see a wood-paneled room. My hands go to my neck. There's no noose, not even the burn of skin rubbed raw with me jerking as I hang from the ceiling. No, I'm standing on solid ground, and this feels too real to be whatever waits to grab you after you die. Too much like what I left behind. I can smell it, the Clorox, the mustiness that has come in waves off of all the bodies that have walked through here. And incense.

It's a chapel.

Behind me is a green door, unlocked. Before me, pews, and a scratched wooden cube for an altar.

In front of the altar, two people: a woman in black slacks and a white button-down shirt, and a chaplain in those same colors. He's got what looks like a portfolio in his hands. I start when I realize it's the same chaplain that pulled me from the line earlier. His face is softer, still wrinkled, but looser. He's smiling.

The chaplain whispers something to the woman, and she sits in the front pew.

They wait in silence for what feels like an uncomfortably long time, a Rikers minute, then the green door opens.

I step to the side, out of sight. I don't know why I'm scared people will see me if this is the afterlife or a dream or something other. But I can't kill instinct, I can only kill myself. So I cling to a shadow. The sound precedes them. The clink of shackles working against themselves. In walks a woman in Rikers beige with a CO holding her arm.

The woman in the pew stands at the sound of the

door slamming shut, looks behind her, and immediately tears start falling down her face.

When the white inmate and the woman in the fancy clothes stand in front of each other by the altar, they hold hands. A strand of blond hair falls from the top-knot on the inmate's head, but she doesn't bother to flick it away. The women can't stop grinning at each other, like the chaplain's joy is contagious. He puts their hands together. *I now pronounce you wife and wife*. The witness, a captain, signs the marriage license the chaplain pulls out of his portfolio.

My ears are buzzing. The world dissolves in a mess of colors. I'm crying.

I try to hang back, deeper into the shadows, but they're certain to see me, and just when they get close enough for me to see the lipstick stain on the inmate's jumpsuit, I'm standing on my bed again, breathing hard.

Deuce, still leaning on the door bars, lifts his head but doesn't look all the way back.

I haven't done it yet. I haven't jumped.

My fingers are shaking, but something is different inside me. Like underground plates shifting, piecing themselves together or breaking apart or both. And suddenly, I don't have the energy anymore. My fingers won't stop shaking, and when Deuce looks back, for real this time, the features of his face slacken. I can't keep my bottom lip from trembling. I can't move. I don't know how he knows to do this, but he walks back over and grabs me by the waist while my trembling fingers work the noose over my head. He lets me back down and I fall forward. He doesn't push me away. He doesn't cuss me out. He doesn't size me up for a beating. He holds me, and what the fuck kind of place is this that can let me cry into this big nigga's shoulder about my mama dying?

—

Banging wakes me up. Soon as I open my eyes, nothing but white. I know by now that it's a flashlight. Brightest flashlight in the world. And my body moves before my mind does. I got ten minutes to get dressed. But I'm up and stretch out the pain in my back, and, in a few moments, I'm in my prison sweats.

In the beginning, being escorted by a guard down to the isolation cells at 1:30 in the morning would mean there was only pain waiting for me at the end. I'd been singled out for a beating or I was going into AdSeg on a write-up or some other horrible thing was about to happen. But I'm on my way to a job, and that kind of knowledge puts a strange feeling in a man. When you have purpose that doesn't involve hurting someone else, it changes the way you walk. I'm not moving through here with a bounce in my step, nothing like that. But I don't have the same tension knotting up my shoulders. I don't have my head ducked and arms loose and ready for when I gotta swing on someone. You let that go when you're on your way to work.

I get to the wing and in the anteroom, I strip down for the cavity search. Then, sweats back on, I'm in the corridor with a few of the guards, one of which is asleep with a contraband magazine on his belly. The one who's awake looks up and gives me a perfunctory nod before returning to whatever part of the wall he was staring at before I came in.

My chair's ready for me in front of the first cell. The cell door has bars enough for me to see through, but even if it didn't, the lights are all the way on in the suicide ward. Nevernight, it gets called. And they say they keep the lights on because then guards can better see when an inmate on suicide watch is going to try something, but keeping someone in that nightmare from being able to sleep ain't gonna help. It ain't my place to tell them that, and a bunch of the guards, the smarter ones, probably know that already, but it ain't their place to say it either.

I take my seat and watch the kid on the other side of the bars not stir in his suicide blanket. Sturdy, quilted, tear-proof nylon. I've seen others where it's been turned into a smock. This collarless, sleeveless gown with adjustable shoulder openings and another opening down the front that gets closed with fasteners. That ain't what this kid got, thank God. It's just the blanket. The way he lies on his mattress, though, it's like he's dead already. But this is my job now: sit with suicidal prisoners and just talk.

So that's what I do.

Introduce myself: name, no NYSID number, then make some crack about how "I didn't do it" or something like that, not because it matters at this point but because, for the younger cats, maybe it helps to hear it come up. I used to talk about how shitty the food was but then I would remember what I used to get when I was in the Box, and I'd remember that their shit probably has worms in it. So instead, I tell him about the others. I tell him about Rick, who's practically an institution he's been here so long, and I talk about Bobby, who did a bid at Folsom in California and used to be a vegetable smuggler, like he actually worked on a garden with some other inmates on China Hill and they would sneak food back into the prison in their clothes: a jalapeño pepper wrapped in a sandwich bag and smushed in his left boot and in his right boot a bundle of tightly wrapped green onion shoots. One guy brought back a watermelon slice, another some tomatoes. And I tell the kid now about what Bobby once told me, which is that they weren't supposed to garden *per se,* they were landscapers, but they weren't gonna *not* garden on that grassy knoll.

And then I tell this kid who may or may not be asleep about the book club.

It's not just a story about a buncha niggas reading a book but it's also a story of some of those niggas being cats locked up for a backpack and some of those niggas being neo-Nazis. A story that makes you ask what's the point of a neo-Nazi learning to treat a black person as a human if he's just gonna die in a year and a half anyway, or maybe the lesson is that the only whites ready to look at black folk as human are the ones getting ready to die anyway. But then I chime in on this conversation I'm having out loud to myself, and say Rikers is weird like that. Jail's weird like that. Prison's weird like that. All types of absurd shit happens here, and you just need the patience to step back and watch it happen. Maybe that comes with time. Maybe not. Maybe you spend your entire sentence here getting the shit kicked outta you. Maybe they kill you in here. But maybe you make it out. Not out from behind bars, but out of wherever it is they try to put you when they put you behind bars.

I'm telling the kid about how everyone in the book

club had to sit at separate tables, and you had to swivel around to talk to people so nobody felt left out. And if someone wanted to read something out of the book, you had to toss it to them and hope they caught it or it landed within reach.

"How long you been here?"

The kid's so quiet that anybody not trained to listen for any little noise might have missed it, but I stop dead in the middle of my sentence.

"You sound like you been here long." He's drugged up. His words slur. He's got that wooziness in him, drunk-tired.

"You just see a lot here pretty quickly," I tell him. But then I add it all up. The arrest, the time in Central Booking, then my arrival at Rikers. Me trying to get my case tried separately from the niggas I was with at the time. Seventy-four days later is the first time I see a judge, and I hear my charges for the first time. Mama wasn't there. Ella wasn't there. But I knew it'd kill them both if I pled guilty, so I tell the room "not guilty," and I get a trial date for six months after that. Two hundred and fifty-eight days later, I'm in court again, bigger from what RNDC has already done to me, and the prosecutor requests a deferment. "People Not Ready" like it takes more than just the DA to do what needs doing to me. Then more deferments, such that I ain't even need to be in court. Two weeks, one week, one week, two weeks. Then fights with inmates and time in the Box and admin charges added to what ain't even technically a sentence, and it blurs. In that blur are more fights, COs attacking us, COs trying to rape us, beating us in the showers, us fighting back, slashing, trying to get our ass-whoopings caught on camera. More time in the Box. "Eight years."

"That's gotta be some sort of record."

I'm stunned. I'd never counted it out like that before. Makes me gulp and need to take a few deep breaths. "Yeah. But I'm getting out soon." I don't say I'm eligible for parole or that I got a hearing coming up, because there ain't enough certainty in those sentences. I need to say I'm getting out. The kid needs to hear that it's possible.

I need to hear that it's possible.

"I'm getting out."

The CO who's still awake taps his shock-stick against the ground. Time's up. I move my chair to the next cell and start talking.

The closer to Kev's parole hearing they get, the more exaggerated his moods. Either he's electric with hypomania or catatonic with depression. Their first of the two hugs they're allotted is swift. Perfunctory. They sit down less like a sister traveling to visit her inmate brother and more like prospective business partners.

Kev fiddles with his fingers, forearms resting heavy on the table, his brows so furrowed they nearly cover his eyes.

Twice he tries to start speaking, but something swallows the words in his throat. Finally, "I wish I'd talked to Mama more."

Confusion and sorrow war in Ella. She blinks her surprise, then flexes her toes.

Strands of white light peel out of thin air and wrap around her, spawning more threads, tree-branching until whole cloth covers her, bathes her in ivory that takes the sun's light and makes her glow.

This is a new thing. Ella takes Kev's hand and smiles. "Come with me, Kev. I want to show you something."

Two steps forward take them into a field overgrown by weeds where, in the distance, railroad tracks cut through overgrowth. A ghost train, translucent against the blue sky, thunders past and Kev squints and sees in one of the compartments, a family, laden with a single suitcase, and sees within that suitcase the clothes and the bags of chicken that are meant to sustain the two children on their journey northward. He doesn't know how he knows they are heading north, nor does he know how he knows where they stand, that it is the Delta, but the conviction rocks him. He watches in wonder as the train passes, its billowing smoke outlined in luminescence by the golden orb that gilds everything its light touches.

They walk through the fields. By now, Ella has let go of Kev's hand, but Kev follows, trusting his older sister to lead him to security, to answers, to certainty. At a vacant lot, a still pool of water fills a parking lot so that the buildings lining the lot see their undisturbed reflections, the auto body shop whose sign is missing half its lettering, the red brick factory building hollowed out into nothing more than a husk with its broken windows like a tiger's teeth. Telephone lines on which stand a murder of crows, the poles untouched but bulging with captured moisture. They walk further to find empty houses that stand in defiance of all natural law, the cement of sidewalks peeled away to reveal the toll of the battle waged between concrete and grassland. Paved roads made brown where the asphalt has vanished. Clouds swim above them. The buildings, homes, warehouses, a courthouse, all of it wears a coat of brown, varying shades, the color of sand or the color of mud, but all brown. The entire town coated in it.

If you hear the dogs, keep going. If you see torches in the woods, keep going. If there's shouting after you, keep going. Don't ever stop. Keep going. If you want a taste of freedom, keep going.

A river runs.

Two hundred miles long and sixty miles wide, cutting through nineteen counties, its ebb and flow enriching the land it touches such that wealth could grow straight out of the topsoil that runs more than sixty feet deep, pregnant with life and black bodies. On the outskirts of the town, along a lonely stretch of road, phantasmal stalks of corn sprout, row after row after row, with spectral farming machinery, rusted and pitted, hanging over the entire enterprise.

The church is plain and white, and if Kev squints, he can see the cracks and rifts in the white paint of its steeple. But from where they stand, the place looks untouched, neat and orderly while the overgrown cemetery behind it holds tombstones like more broken teeth. Wisps of smoke rise from the air to become silhouettes of people working a field while a plantation house builds itself, ghostly tendril by ghostly tendril, out of the ground on its hilltop perch. Streams of black folk dressed in Sunday white flow in and out of the church. Mothers with their gloved hands holding their children's. Husbands with their elbows out for their wives to wrap their arms through. Silent, but Kev strains to hear the giggling and the chatter and the warmth and the love nonetheless. Ella stoops as a ghost child comes by her and reaches out to touch the child's cheek only to have it melt around her finger, then her hand, then vanish completely.

Dusk breeze cuts through the vision, and the people disappear, so that all that remains is the church. The heat settles on their shoulders like a blanket. Gnats and mosquitoes sing all over their legs and fingers.

A step forward, and they cross so much ground that Kev falls to his knees, sick, and finds he is kneeling in water. His head darts left and right, and he knows without knowing how he knows that it's the Yazoo River that darkens his DOC-issued orange jumpsuit.

Looking up, he sees more ghosts. A minister with one hand cupped over a woman's nose and mouth and another pressed against the small of her back, their waists rising out of the water, their white gowns pooled around them, and the minister dipping the woman back like they were dancing and no one else could see them, then bringing her back up out of the water, her gown soaked through and clinging to her angles and curves, her black hair curled and clumped about her ears and neck, her skin a-sheen, and Kev knows without knowing how he knows that he and that woman share blood. His hands go to his face, fingertips shivering against cheeks wet with tears. Then the wind takes the ghosts from them, and Kev's gasp catches in his chest, and he stares while that spot transforms into a street in downtown Greenwood, two lone black boys in suspenders with books slung by straps over their shoulders, talking like no one else can hear them, none of the white store proprietors staring out through their windows or the man showing his neighbor's son the contents of his toolbox, the box itself splayed open on a front porch. None of the girls walking back from school with their mothers suddenly wrapping them into forced silence with their arms, pulling them away so that wherever the black boys who share his blood go, the rest of the world spread apart from them, until the road empties and all that can be heard is the car that races toward them, full of white boys holding bats and chains, in full pursuit of the young black men who had dared to walk through their part of town without their permission. Kev knows what happens after without knowing how he knows: that the two boys, cousins to each other, have found sanctuary in a nearby river and how they nearly drown for holding their breath so long while the white boys with their lights search the bank, then the daring black boys getting home with their chests heaving from panic and effort to face a mother, an aunt, livid, purple with worry.

The images spin into stories, so many stories, so that he sees another young man working under the sun as a sharecropper on a plantation, finding a bumpy log on which to sit, taking his hat off and running his forearm along his forehead, then finding the water pump and pouring some into his hat's brim to splash on his head and face. The overseer comes out without his whip because why would he need it? And from the porch, he shouts at the man on the log, and it's as if Kev's in the dream, he can't hear the words only see the white mouth contort in disgust around them. The black man stands up, not quite to his full height, but instead of turning back to his hoe, he turns to the overseer and says something back. Kev can't hear the words, but he can see the words straighten the man's back, can see each syllable building pride inside him, and he's not angry, he just wants the rest he's earned. The wind churns, and it's dusk, and the young man who dared to rest has fled to his grand-aunt's clapboard house and his grand-uncle girds himself with a Winchester rifle and a long-nose .38, and sets on the front porch waiting for the mob to come after a man who dared to assert his worth.

The ritual: a social code broken, then fleeing to the sanctuary of family members who gather to protect the loved one on the run, the loved one now in danger, until plans can be made, slapped together, to spirit that person up north.

The ground falls out from beneath Kev. When he

opens his eyes, he and Ella are standing on air. Ella looks as though she has not moved this entire time, as though she were a piece of furniture or a tree having withstood all manner of storm. Staring at this woman, Kev realizes what he has seen and feels anger and jealousy that this woman has gained access to more of their mother's life than Kev had ever been granted, that so much of the mystery of Mama has been solved.

Shotgun shacks and unpaved roads and cotton fields. Young men "progueing," strutting around and being seen, and rivers swollen with black bodies. Patchwork streetlamp grid that turns some neighborhoods into lightless blocks, churches set up to register neighborhood denizens to vote with lines stretching out the entrance and down the block and those churches being reduced to splinters on a night where it didn't matter if there were people in it or not, just that what they wanted to say got said. A man putting on a white hood and mounting a horse and galloping to an agitator's house to light a cross on fire on that front lawn, burn a crucifix into that grass when the wood falls, then finding himself the next morning at the State Capitol in a bespoke suit debating the merits of a piece of legislation. Men turned into pieces of meat, having been dragged by a car or a truck down backstreets where mosquitoes and alligators and gutter snakes roam. The smell of

sweet barbecue sauce wafting up from a grill in a back-
yard while uncles and aunts slapped at their necks or
their legs and where kids scurried underneath chairs or
flirted or did the things people do when they're no longer unfree.

"Mama," Kev whispers.

He reaches a hand out and takes a step toward one
of the little pig-tailed girls being bounced on an older
woman's knee.

"Mama." Tears blur the vision. "Mama. Oh, Mama."

It feels like forever, but it was only a few seconds.
And in the visiting room, Ella sneaks her hand away before the guard can catch her.

Across the table, Kev smiles his thanks. Tears still
pool in his eyes, and he lets them rest there for a moment before sniffing them away and becoming his hard
self again.

"They're really gonna let me out, aren't they." When
Kev says it, it doesn't sound like a question. It doesn't
sound like an acclimation. It sounds like an accusation. It
sounds like Kev himself peering sideways into Ella's head,
a passenger in her mind as she spoke with Kev's public
defender and handed over the materials to help the defender make the case for parole with the review board—
the proof of lodging, the contact info for Kev's eventual
employer, the location and admission requirements for

nearby schools. It sounds like Kev watching her brush past every correctional officer whose path she crossed, grazing just enough to let her Thing flow through them and convince them of what a model inmate Kev has been. It sounds like Kev watching Ella cheat.

"When you get out," Ella asked. "Where do you wanna go?"

For a while, he doesn't say anything. Ella watches the potential answers wash across his face, watches him catch them, bounce them from hand to hand or turn them over, then toss them away. Watches him carry in his arms the whole time a simple desire to be away from violence. Until finally he comes to the one word Ella never wanted to hear again.

"West."

IV

WATTS

WATTS is a Sponsored spot.

I didn't really know what that meant until I got out here. The parole board picked it when they put all my shit through the algorithm. My records, my time in Rikers, the stint upstate, my mental health assessment, the Urban Wounded program Ella set me up with out here, job prospects, all of that. I told them I wanted to be out west, away from people, places, and things that'd bring me back to jail, and Watts was the best option that came up. There are Sponsored communities all over the country, and you can tell them where you'd prefer to be and why, like maybe somewhere closer to family or somewhere away from where you have an outstanding beef, and the humans on the parole board will pretend to have the final say, but they pretty much rubberstamp whatever the algo spits out.

I'd worried about pushback. The logistics of having

the System follow me all the way out there, but apparently it wasn't a problem. They got it all figured out. They even contacted a mechanic that'll put me to work right away. No more job applications with the Box on it.

Ella never asks me why I wanted to go out west of all places, and I never ask her why it bothers her so much. I know she and Mama lived out in Florence, in South Central, for a bit before I was born. But I remember I was born there, and it's the only time I can remember both Mama and Ella smiling at me.

Either way, when I get there, I see sprawl. Newly painted stucco houses. Everything's one or two stories. And there's a daytime brilliance to everything, gives it a shine I never got from the crowded, leaning tenements in Harlem. But there are logos everywhere. A large billboard over the Pacific Electric tracks with the same three-bar logo as what was on the machine that told me to come out here. No ankle monitor for me. Instead, after the hearing, they cut my thumb open and put a chip in, which I heard they'd started doing a few years back. No chance of snipping your monitor off or having it malfunction when you go for a swim. While there's now no way to get away with a drink or a hit or a Xanax bar, I don't have to pee in front of a guy I don't know who could send me back to jail if he had a fight with his girl the night before. The chip had the three-bar logo on it before they put it in me.

I walk by the abandoned train tracks and half expect to see bottle shards from when kids come by here, bored, to break something. But there's nothing. No needles, no broken bottles, no empty dime bags. Tin cans, nails, nothing. A couple blocks away, kids play on a jungle gym.

A part of me expected post-apocalypse when I got here. On the inside, you hear about what's going on outside, new presidents elected, rise in hate crimes. Nazis in the streets killing black folk. Folks getting locked up for whatever again. Important shit getting lit on fire. You remember the old heads in jail telling you about riots in the '60s, riots in the '90s. Younger cats my age telling me about the riots in the 2010s. What's left after all of that? Pigeons congregating on the red-tiled roof of a police substation, vacant lots still charred around the edges, shards of broken port bottles winking at you in the sun. All types of refugee-type kids walking barefoot with pieces of glass in the bottoms of their feet, not even flinching because living through the End of the World enough times does that to you.

But, no. They got pool halls here and churches. Mosques, even. It's like one of those Rockwell paintings but if a hood nigga stood over his shoulder whispering in his ear about home.

But this ain't home; at least, no home I'm trying to get back to. It looks new. All of it. Which suits me just fine.

━━━━━━

My place is one of those one-stories on a block of identical houses. There's a yard and a chain-link fence. Even space for a garden, but I guess they're leaving it up to me to see if I want to plant something. I half expect to see niggas out on their front lawns riding those big-ass lawnmowers you see white dudes riding in the movies, all moving in unison on some *Stepford Wives*–type shit. But it's all quiet. A few folks hang out on their front porches. One or two nurse a cold beer. And the sun sits on the horizon so that the whole sky is cut with knife scars of purple and pink and white and blue.

I go to the knob, but when I try to turn it, it doesn't budge. There's no keyhole. Curtains cover the windows so I can't see inside, and I call up the info on my Palm, and it says I'm at the right spot. I'm geotagged where I'm supposed to be. This is the address.

They said stuff like this was supposed to be over now that we didn't have to deal with real actual human beings anymore, just algorithms and machines, and I figured the parole board was the last set of ugly-ass white faces I'd have to see for the rest of my life, but if I have to call in tech support for this bullshit in my first week?

I can feel it building. Even as I know it's coming and I know what it'll mean, the world begins to take on a shade of red, and I'm two steps away from breaking my fists against these Plexiglas windows when I hear "Youngblood!" from behind me.

He's got one of those older-man short-sleeve button-downs, the type that come cut specifically to accommodate the basketball-belly you get once you hit forty. He's got a beer in his hand, fingers only half covering the O'Douls label.

He's chuckling. That kind of chuckle that old heads let out when they see something they think reminds them of themselves. If it ain't the most irritating sound in the world, it's close. "You gotta use the touchpad."

"Touchpad?"

With his beer, he points to a small black square right by where a doorbell would usually go.

"They gave you a keycard, right?"

"You on parole too?" I realize he's the first dude I've talked to since I got here. Maybe this place looks so new because it's a ghost town. Ain't nobody get here yet.

"Yeah, three years now."

"Where you from?"

"Florissant." Meaning St. Louis. Meaning the South. The way he says it, he knows I'm supposed to give him respect now. It ain't enough to be an old head anymore or to have the tattooed proof that you were out once, banging, or that you were doing any number of other foolish things. Bringing the Fury or the Force or whatever it's called where you come from down on your head out of your own stupidity. But some places, you got to deal with the worst of white folk, the terrorists. The places that made money off you by charging you for tickets and scheduling court dates when they knew you couldn't make it, then fining you for those missed dates if they don't jail you first, then they say they'll graciously set you up with a payment plan, then you get a day or two late one month and they put out a warrant, then when they do get you in jail, you gotta post $2,000 bond or some shit like that that they know you can't pay, and that's how it starts. While in jail, you miss your job interview, and when you finally get your day in court, they say you gotta change out of your jumpsuit, but you gotta put on the same funky clothes you spent however long getting arrested in and you gotta stand in that courtroom smelling like rotten poom-poom, handcuffed, and you gotta do all you can to even feel like a person still. If you got family, maybe your mama can borrow against her life insurance policy to post your bond.

I know better than to ask him about kids.

He's at my side now, and out of his back pocket, he pulls a thin white card. Whatever writing used to be imprinted on it is pretty faded. Looks like Braille more than anything else, but it's got the three-bar logo on it.

"Each house here got one of those touchpads. Put this to it, and you're golden."

I pat my pockets. I don't remember getting anything that looked like that, not at Rikers and not here, and now I'm back to getting ready to cuss out the System that can't even get rid of me properly. "I ain't get that," I tell him. Then I remember something. "They put a chip in my thumb, though."

The dude's eyebrows rise in slight surprise. "Ain't that some shit." After a beat, "Well, go on. Try it!"

I put my thumb to the touchpad, and the screen door slowly opens toward us. Then the main door slides into the wall, revealing a room dressed in darkness. But already, I can make out a couch, a dining room table with chairs around it, and a hallway, which must probably lead to a bedroom and a bathroom. It's strange to think of those two things as being separate. Feels, more than any of this other stuff, like the greatest luxury in the world. I ain't gotta shit where I sleep.

"Who's paying for this?" I ask, without turning back to face him.

"You are, Youngblood," the dude says, laughing outright. "Nigga, who you think?"

"How, though?"

"Same way everybody else does. They take it out your paycheck." He's shaking his head at me while I take the whole thing in. It hadn't really hit me till then. Barely do I get to process my freedom before I already got another set of obligations sitting on my shoulders. But this is good. In prison, in jail, routine was good. Had three square meals a day, though most days you couldn't call 'em that. Had work. Also had to remember that you never knew when or where the harm would come from.

But I look around, and I only see the two of us on this street. And it doesn't sound like anybody's waiting for me in there.

"It's all right," he tells me. "You ain't incarcerated no more."

I wanna tell him I know, but it'd be a lie.

He starts to walk away. "Next time you in trouble, need some help, call on Calvin."

———

There's more room in the shop than I think Miguel needs. It's supposed to be a barbershop-type setup, but we're in an open hangar, a bunch of us with varying degrees of time on the outside. Royce came up in Detroit and was in Dearborn for a while before getting transferred here. Romero was the Dominican from the Bronx, Marlon the Jamaican from the same neighborhood. They hadn't known each other growing up, had gone to the same high school and mixed it up with the same gangs but never really banged with each other until after they got out and had that whole "Hey, ain't you the cat from—" exchange.

There's metal all around us. It's gotten hot enough outside that you can't let your skin touch the hoods of the rusted-out car-husks scattered out around the hangar. A couple other parolees lie on them anyway, knees up, newspapers covering their faces as they try to sleep. We're supposed to be working, but a bunch of us don't have our mechanic's license yet, so we have to apprentice. And Miguel's only got one customer right now.

A light-skinned man sits quietly in his chair, chest up against a cushion, his stub of a right arm out on another cushion in front of him. Miguel has his tools on a piece of metal at the man's arm, and sparks spray in arcs that sizzle when they hit the floor. Miguel used to be a barber and a tattooist, and now he does this.

"There's no union or anything like that yet," the light-skinned dude in the chair is saying, "but a bunch of us at the factory are trying to get something together."

"You think they'll allow it?" asks Miguel almost absentmindedly in that way barbers have of maintaining conversation while engaging in the geometric precision required for a fly high-top fade.

Marlon leans forward on his milk crate. "You just can't call it a union in English. You gotta say it in Spanish. Or patois. Had a PO one time who thought bumbaclots were an after-school snack for the kids. Like fuckin' Tostinos pizza rolls or some shit."

Mero lets out his belly laugh and nearly falls off his own crate. "Make their software in their fuckin' algorithm auto-translate from Spanish to English and the shit still doesn't make sense."

"Right! Dominican Spanish ain't Spanish, my nigga. It's Dominican-ese. It's like in the Pen when you gotta speak that code while your shorty visiting."

Mero pointed his O'Douls at Marlon. "But she gotta sag her pants when she first come in because the CO's like 'No, ma, you can't come in here, you look too sexy right now' or she gets turned away 'cause she got the underwire in her bra."

Marlon chuckles. "Right before she pulls the heroin out her poom-poom."

Even that gets me laughing.

Mero lets out a sigh and says, "Shoutout to jail."

"No!" Marlon shouts back. "Shoutout to getting out!"

Royce, on the car hood, removes the paper from his face, then slides so his legs dangle over the side. He doesn't even flinch when the hot, rotted metal touches his skin, makes me think he's got augments, or prosthetics at least. "Niggas really think when you get out, you just gonna start over. Niggas never stopped. You ever play Monopoly, my nigga? You know how you go to jail, then you just wait two turns or whatever? Wait till I get out, I'ma buy Baltic Ave., nigga. Niggas couldn't walk down Boardwalk without paying respect."

He says it all straight-faced, but we know he's clowning.

"Everything green was me, nigga."

Mero says, "You know all the avenues in Monopoly are mad fucked up in real life. You know that, right?"

Marlon: "You can actually buy those avenues with Monopoly money." Through his laughter, "Bronx Monopoly."

Meanwhile, I'm staring at the guy in the chair. He's chuckling while Miguel's saying something to him, but I can't hear any of it. "Ayo!" I call out. "What's that factory job like? Is it government?"

Marlon giggles. "You see how he asked that question?

Like it was pino or something. Oooh, look at that nigga workin' weekends getting that double-overtime. Weekend rates, hunh, my dick is hard, yo."

Mero: "Damn, you know how much vacation time that nigga probably accruing?"

"You don't even look at girls and shit, you like, 'You know that nigga got benefits, right? Oooh, I wonder what that nigga paystub look like.' Wake up in the morning with your robe open, watching the sanitation workers."

I have to wait for the Bronx niggas to calm down before I can nod at the dude in the barber's chair. "So?"

The dude in the chair shrugs. "I'm here getting a new arm."

"You lose the old one workin'?"

"Yeah, but the Sponsors got me covered. Paid for my hospital time and everything."

Mero leans forward on his crate. "They ain't dock your pay?"

The dude winks as Miguel fuses the metal to the man's nerves. "Government job, yo."

"Issa Babylon ting," Marlon murmurs in an exaggerated Rasta accent, smirking.

I squint. "That don't hurt?"

The dude lets loose another shrug. Not sure if he's trying hard to advertise for these factory jobs. Maybe he's getting paid to seem as excited for this gig as he reasonably can. "Nah, the Company turns off the pain receptors for my appointment. My chip, yo."

I look at my thumb, where my own chip was put in after the parole board back in New York approved my release. Can't tell if it's the way the sun's shining and casting shadows, but I think I see it glowing blue under my skin. Blue bars like the Company logo I seen on the billboards.

———

There's a bunch of us in a circle.

Dr. Bissell's the one with his back to the door, and the rest of us sit around him. About eight of us or so. Almost all black and brown. Nobody's got gang tats, so it's like we were all singles passing through the system, spat out to land here in this little oasis where we have a job and a pretty big place to sleep. Dr. Bissell doesn't say much. Looks like he's been doing these sessions for a while, and he's seen enough of us come through that he knows it's impossible to "earn" our respect, like a points system or something, but that sometimes you just gotta let the one guy talk and the others'll maybe slide through that open door. I remember the prison counselors and all those mental health workers Rikers used to churn through. Just couldn't shut the fuck up and stick around to wait and see that these closed-down, shut-down niggas just lookin' for a reason, any reason, to talk.

Calvin's here too. Tan-color button-down over his Jupiter-sized belly.

"Violence causes trauma," Calvin had told me just before I slid through the open door to this room. "And trauma causes violence, Youngblood. Hurt people hurt people." He'd said it in a low, counseling voice. I wanted to tell him to stop calling me Youngblood. Twenty-eight ain't that young.

A kid named Davis is talking. Philly kid. Probably the kind of shooter Philly rappers rapped about know-ing personally. The ones they were whipping work in the kitchen with, maybe the type to appear in their music videos. If I pulled up a Meek or Beanie or Cassidy music video on someone's tablet, I'd maybe see him neon-lit in the background.

"It's like, we don't get shot or stabbed, we get ourselves shot or stabbed, you know?" He talks with his hands in front of him, constantly putting his fist in his palm for emphasis. That's the whole ambit of his reach. He doesn't wave, doesn't point, just claps with his knuckles and palms. "Like, my boy—I ain't gonna say his name—but after he got shot and got out the ER, he used to jump out in front of buses and, at the last minute, hold his hands out." Soft clap. "I ain't wanna end up like that. So soon as I could, I got the transfer to Watts. I heard you was here." He shakes his head. "And all over some stupid shit."

An Atlanta cat named Hendrix, with dreads down past his shoulders, leans back in his chair. Type of nigga to wear sunglasses indoors. "You ever think about revenge?"

Davis bristles. "All the time, nigga. What you think?"

Their voices have started to rise, and I eye Dr. Bissell, who remains unmoved.

"That's why I come here. So I can talk about it, 'stead of do it. What I look like, huntin' the nigga who stabbed me over weed."

I feel Ella in the room. Standing somewhere between me and Davis. Haunting me. And her Thing, her ability to get into other people's heads, it's starting to get to me, so that when Davis talks about the nigga who stabbed him over weed, I can see the abandoned church on the corner of 18th and Ridge in North Central Philly, and I can see Davis taking too long to mull over a purchase and the other dude, bulky Sixers jacket on to protect against the Philly winter, sucking his teeth, getting impatient, then telling Davis to go buy his weed elsewhere in a few more words than that and Davis saying, "I go wherever the fuck I wanna go," and the dude saying some things back, then Davis swinging and catching

147

the dude on the side of his head, and the dude swinging and Davis not caring if the dude was strapped, just knowing that if he got the drop fast enough, he could smack the dogshit outta dude, but then metal glints—a knife—and the other dude slashes then stabs, and then Davis watching the knife going in and out in and out in and out, still swinging, feeling no pain, even though there's blood everywhere, then the dude running out of Davis's grip and Davis writhing on the ground, then Davis thinking of calling an ambulance, thankful the weedman ain't take his phone, but then realizing he'd have to pay, like, $2,000 so, gritting his teeth, Davis picks himself up and walks a little over a mile to Hahnemann University's emergency department. During the whole walk, Davis is holding his stomach together. Blood drips on the sidewalk. Strangers see him, offer to help. But his Francisville folk, the people he's known all his life, know better than that. They know what kind of person he is. So he shrugs off the strangers and walks and walks and walks.

And I wake up, still in the circle with the other Watts guys. Everybody's quiet, and Davis is looking at me with this pained look in his eyes. I got no idea how long I was out. But I must've been staring the whole time.

I put my hand to my eyes, shake Ella out of my head.

"I'm good," I say quietly. It looks like they're waiting

for me to say more, but I've already lied once to these guys. When Hendrix starts talking about his prison bid and the first time he got thrown in AdSeg, I have to leave. I can't live through that guy's memories too.

———

Dr. Bissell's door is open, but I knock anyway.

He has a tablet on his desk and a few pictures of what I guess are his family. The frames' backs are turned to me, so it's just a guess. He sees me and smiles, then gets up to shake my hand. "Kevin, right?"

"Yeah. Kev. Kevin Jackson."

He goes to close the door, then I sit down in one of the chairs and he takes his seat behind his desk.

"Trouble sleeping," I tell him, before he can keep going with any small talk. "You the type of doctor that can write a prescription or something?"

"We don't do prescriptions here." He folds his hands and leans forward on his desk. His shirtsleeves are rolled up. No tattoos that I can see. Doesn't mean he isn't his own kind of hard. "But if residual anxiety from your time inside is getting to be too much, I can write to the Company and have them up your dosage."

"Dosage? Of what?"

"They gave you an implant, correct?"

I look at my thumb. "You mean this? Yeah, but it's only for access. You know, to my home and stuff. And when they need to check on me."

"Well, the chips are also equipped to monitor your biorhythms, and when the chemicals in your brain begin to show signs of rising anxiety levels or if your symptoms of PTSD begin to recur, it can release chemicals to counteract them. Are your episodes recent?"

I shrug. I'd dreamt of the night I borrowed Freddie's ski mask. "I mean, I had one last night, but it's never really been that bad."

He doesn't say anything for a while. "Do you remember how many times you were in solitary confinement? It's all right if you don't."

I chuckle nervously, because I don't know how else to react. "I mean, the days kind of blend together in AdSeg. Look, there anything you can do to, like, up the dosage or something? I'm not trying to remember all of that." My heart rate's rising even while I sit here. "I got a burst of something last night that helped me sleep, but I need more."

"The session was triggering, wasn't it."

"Yeah, but—"

"The chemicals are supposed to be a supplement, not the entire treatment." He pauses to consider me. "Here is all about making you a productive member of society.

Giving you a chance to contribute." It sounds like a speech he's done many times, but he also sounds like the type of nigga to make it seem like every time is the first time he's done it. "Getting you back on your feet. Now, I'm sure there's a lot that happened to you inside that's never going to go away. We can't reverse time. We can't make those things un-happen. We can, however, move forward. And we can teach you to avoid triggers. And for those triggers you can't avoid, we can teach you to deal with them."

It's not what I'm here to hear, and he sees it. "I . . . I have a sister. Ella." Even as I talk, as I sound out the idea, it sounds strange to mention her to someone else. I don't think I'd said her name to anyone that wasn't family in nearly a decade. "Having a supportive family helps people not go back in, you know. And I was wondering, if I can reach her, can she visit? Like we used to do in jail?"

Dr. Bissell's face drops. Like I punched him in the chest. "She can't."

Before I know it, the anger's got ahold of me, but I grip the armrests and keep the rage right there in my fingers.

"This is a Sponsored community. Outsiders not a part of the program are not permitted." He looks off into the middle distance. "There's been trouble in the past. Some folks haven't been able to deal with parts of their past that come here to see them. This is about a new start. Completely blank slate."

"Till my parole's over. In three years."

Dr. Bissell cracks his knuckles. His nervous tic. "I'll write to the Company about upping your dosage."

I know this man's here to help me. And I know he's doing the best he can. He has a job, and it comes with constraints, and he's trying to help me the only way he knows how, but that doesn't stop my bloody thoughts.

It hits with the same suddenness as last night. That wave of peace. I ain't have to look at my thumb to know it's glowing. But I exhale and tap the armrests. "It's all right. I'm good," I tell him. This time, it's only half a lie.

———

The stars are out by the time I get home. So's Calvin.

He has a rocking chair out front. "You got time to rap for a minute, Youngblood?"

I don't want to try sleeping just yet, so I walk over to him, post up on his porch. He's got a six-pack of O'Douls Cherry, fishes one out and hands it to me, but I wave it away. "I don't drink." No more. And for a while, we sit there in silence. The only sound is his chair squeaking underneath him while he rocks. No one's shouting from their cells. No COs are barking orders. There's no mysterious banging from everywhere and nowhere at once. No sirens. No stampede of bootsteps as the Riot Squad clears the wing. Nobody's blasting reggaeton from their windows. Niggas always talked about how the quiet was the thing that eventually got to them, how that was the most difficult thing to cope with, but only now do I know what they mean. There are maybe a few other ex-cons on the block now, some of them moved in about a week ago, but I can't even hear cicadas anymore.

"This don't feel like prison to you?" I ask Calvin. Shit comes out of my mouth without my knowing more and more these days. I hate it.

"Whatchu mean?"

I wave at the houses lining the street. "We completely shut off. No family comes to see us. I can't use Facebook. No Twitter, no YouTube, nothing. I'm cut off. I wake up, I watch Miguel work until I get a permit to do my own welding, I go to my weekly meetings with Dr. Bissell, everything's an appointment. And there's no option to not do it, because there's shit else to do."

Calvin snorts. "You was happy a month ago." He takes a swig. "And when you start to get upset, they pump that chemical from your chip into your brains and shit gets square again. You out, Youngblood. When you think about what you can't do, think about what you get to do. You get to earn money."

"I earned money inside, too. I had a job. I fixed computers. How is this any different?"

Calvin gets that look I seen older heads on the block get when they know they can't talk sense into the youth.

I think I hate Watts.

———————

I sometimes feel her behind my eyes, trying to bring me somewhere else when I'm working on prosthetics with Miguel or some other odd shape of metal, and I get nothing but pain from her. Any old thing makes her cry these days. And then I resent her for it. I dread every visit. The heart gets going, and heat flushes my face, and it's like I'm getting ready to fight someone I can't throw a punch at, so I just gotta stand there and take this new rage she's got inside her, and that's when I see some of where she's been spending her time: the auditorium of Chicago's public-safety headquarters where members of the police board sit beneath a banner that reads: "Chicago Police Generations—a Proud Family Tradition." And the men at the front of the room are white, almost translucent. Like holograms, and the black folk in the audience are real and sweating and hurting and vivid with hypertension and the club and the church, and one woman is up on her feet shouting, "We know this board doesn't care about black women! We know this board doesn't care about black people!" As the police board tries in vain to explain upgrades to the algorithm that has been powering their policing, the algorithm developed in conjunction with extremely smart people in Silicon Valley, and that has helped reduce crime in the South Side by 19 percent, "But that's raised the number of black boys you lock up without pretext by 200 percent," another black woman shouts back.

"Listen to black women!" a young man in the audience shouts from his seat, half in jest, and everyone's cheering and clapping, for him and for the woman still standing.

Then the police killings. The mechanized cops programmed with this supposedly race-neutral algorithm. And outside Watts, a dozen more shootings produce a dozen more weeping families that have to struggle stoically through their black grief or that can stand behind microphones and declare their black anger, and the bodies pile higher and higher and higher, and so does the frustration with the impunity "because," says the district attorney in St. Louis in Kansas City in Staten Island in Dayton in Gary in Albuquerque in Oakland, "you can't indict an algorithm."

I see Ella walking through Milwaukee's North Side, past makeshift memorials to dead black kids: teddy bears, browning flowers, ribbons tied to telephone poles waving in the breeze, and I know that she's been touching the ground around those memorials and closing her eyes and seeing the whole of it, whether the bullet came from some other colored kid's gun or from a cop, watching the whole story unfold before her.

She does the same with the Confederate monuments that rise from the ground in the South like weeds. Tributes to treasonous generals and soldiers serving Big Cotton. She touches their bases, feels their mass-produced faces, runs her fingers over their inscriptions. She wants to know who was hanged here. Who was beaten here. In whose name they were violated.

She's gathering it within her. All of it.

———

The turret guns follow Ella as she walks up the sidewalk. Everyone who would have tended to the concrete is indoors or has fled the neighborhood for a place where Guardians don't circle overhead, where surveillance orbs don't scan their faces and match their features against their recorded data, where Augments don't congregate on sidewalks, outside of shops, at subway entrances, to disappear anyone with a record. The young whites who have moved in, some of them carrying about them the faint whiff of weed in their dirty dreadlocks, turn their heads when they see her, then turn back around when she gets out of earshot. It's a short walk, but it feels like a pilgrimage across a desert.

She gets to the church, and it stands out like a single, manicured toenail in a gangrenous foot. A single thought, and the door pushes open. The hinges have been oiled, she can tell, but the doors still make a ponderous sound when they move and when they close behind her.

A single man in rolled-up shirtsleeves slips hymnals under the pews.

For a moment, a feeling of transgression shoots through her. She feels like an interloper. Then it passes, and she's able to step forward, loud enough to be heard.

The man raises his head, salt-and-pepper beard trimmed close to his jawline. He smiles, tired. "Bible study ain't tonight, it's tomorrow."

"I know, Pastor. I just—"

Worry creases his brow, and she knows he's thinking about the Guardians. He's thinking of the algorithms that police the block and wondering if this break in the pattern of movement will bring them down on his head.

She doesn't know why she's here. Maybe if I wait long enough, this man can tell me, she tells herself. "You— my mother used to come here. Her name was Elaine."

The worry vanishes, replaced by the joy that comes

with time-traveling to an aureate memory. "Lanie," he says, wistfully. Then sorrow darkens his features. "So sorry for your loss. Wow, you must be Ella." He seems to forget the police forces outside. "It's been so long. You live around here now?"

Ella shrugs.

"Here, take a seat." He sits on the cushioned pew and pats the space next to him.

They sit in religious silence.

"Your mother was one of our most enthusiastic members. No matter how many shifts at the hospital she had to work, she came through. Some Sundays, she was even wearing her scrubs!"

Ella imagines those Sundays, Mama on the subway heading here straight from work, not even bothering to wake up her children, Kev revealing later that Mama had been texting him the whole time to keep tabs on his sister, to make sure she was getting her rest, to see if she'd broken anything, if she'd broken herself.

"She even headed her own Bible study." He chuckles.

"You still get churchgoers?"

He rocks back and forth on the pew. "It's not how it used to be. Everyone's older or moved out. Some of the new residents come by, but few stay. These new kids, they don't seem to have much need for what's on offer here, but we keep on keepin' on. That's what we do, right?"

"Is it?" There's bite in her voice. Too much bite.

He lets the moment settle. "You had a brother, right? Kevin?"

"Yeah. He's out on parole."

The pastor nods, putting the pieces together in his mental timeline. "Lanie used to bring him. Had him taking notes in that pew right over there. Probably to keep him awake more than anything else. But he'd walk in with that notebook and his glasses, and he'd be scribbling down all the points I was making in my sermons. Put quite a bit of pressure on me to get it right, if I'm being honest. Sometimes, after the service, I'd see his notes. He had bullet points and everything. She knew how that child worked. She was getting him to try organizing"— he waves his hand to indicate the human entirety—"all of this. How to fit grace and tribulation into the same cupboard. Probably figured that child's strongest muscle was his brain." He leans over to Ella and says, in a conspiratorial whisper, "But it's the heart."

"Do you worry, Pastor?"

"About?"

"About some kid who hates us walking into here and shooting you and your congregation dead?"

The pastor sits back in his pew seat and looks heavenward. "God's will is God's will. But faith is believing not just that He's omniscient and omnipotent, but omnibenevolent as well. Faith is believing that the universe is organized out of love for us." He looks to me. "What that white boy did? Many of us still carry it in us. And I'm not going to tell you to love and forgive it away. It's not my place to tell you how to grieve, but—"

"Stop."

He blinks at her.

"Why can't it happen here?"

"I'm not sure what you—"

"Why can't what happened in Charleston happen here?"

The pastor turns his gaze away and looks again to the altar, like he's searching for guidance. "All we can do is the work. I recognize it's not enough to preach free love. We have to combat free hate as well. You know the story of Sodom and Gomorrah, don't you?"

"Yes."

"Well, for a few years now, I've had a sneaking suspicion that there *were* ten righteous men, only their righteousness was not relevant. That's been the great problem of the church. Pretending that in here is different from out there. For many people, it needs to be."

"When you talk about righteous people, you talkin' about white people?"

He smirks at her. "They ain't *all* bad." Then, he lets out a soft chuckle. "People need to feel safe here."

"That mean gettin' lied to?"

"Child, I don't lie to my congregation." Metal stiffens his voice, and Ella's body sings to it. "We don't get where we're going by matching hate for hate." And in his mind, she sees it. Amid the swirl of fire and screaming and riots, she sees streets packed with factories. Bursting with black life. A man dressed in the suit of an actuary coming out of his house and waving to the factory worker next door. The houses teeming with professionals and gangsters and new homeowners. The pastor, a younger man, eyeing the strip where sits a place with a sign emblazoned: THE CHIT CHAT LOUNGE. And he's got a fedora on his head and a trumpet case in his hand. He joins the folk on the sidewalk and walks past the drugstore and the grocery and the woman opening her drapery-cleaning shop. And then the wig shop for the beauty salon where the street girls went to, not the church ladies who lived a few streets over. And in the air, the word "Detroit." Before it all burned to the ground. "I'm just trying to carry us to the next day." He grits his teeth. "Look at outside. We don't have drug dealers on the corners anymore. I can't remember the last time someone was shot on this block. My churchgoers can come and go in peace."

"When there isn't a curfew. Pastor, this isn't peace. This is order."

His eyes ask her, "And why would we give that up?"

Ella rises to her feet. Whatever she was looking for, she's not gonna get it here. "I was a kid when they let O.J. off. Everyone knew he was guilty. I mean, everyone. Wasn't till I got older that I realized why it happened." He frowns, waiting for her to continue. "Same reason the housing laws got passed in 1968. Same reason we got civil rights in '64."

"Child, what do you know about '64? You weren't even alive back then!"

"But you were!" she shouts back. "You should know. You were in Detroit when the riots happened." Ella calms herself. "They freed the slaves at gunpoint, Pastor." She softens. "My brother, Kev. He was born during the L.A. riots. 1992. Mama and I were trapped in the hospital when it happened. When we came out, everything was gone, but I had a baby brother."

"Violence didn't give you your brother."

Ella grits her teeth and remembers it ain't this church she wants to punish. "But it will get him back."

When she squeezes her eyes closed, she sees Mama in her last moments, a phantom of her former self. She feels so much of Mama's entirety: her history, her love, her bitterness. Lounging on cars with friends in a languid Mississippi summer, mopping blood off a hospital room floor, praying with Ella, for Ella, on a sidewalk in

South Central. All of it, gone. And all Ella could do was watch. This pastor didn't save her. Ella didn't save her. Ella couldn't.

She tries not to turn the wooden doors into splinters on her way out.

It's not till she's outside that she realizes what she was looking for in there. What she's been looking for all these years. What she realizes now she no longer needs.

Permission.

I am the locusts. Ella sends the thought out like a concussive wave, so that it hits every surveillance orb in the neighborhood, every wired cop, every crabtank in the nearby precinct. I am the locusts and the frogs and the rivers of blood.

I'm here now.

———

I'm putting on my watch when I see Ella in front of me, smiling. Her locs are completely silver, not an inch of black in them, and they're floating in the air around her head, almost like a halo.

Before I can tell her not to, Ella makes the room vanish.

Noise. So much noise. Voices shouting at each other, people giving orders, someone crying out in pain.

I'm in a waiting room.

Everybody's clustered beneath the TVs. I turn to Ella. "Where are we?" But the question's barely out of my mouth before I see the grainy footage on one of the televisions. An angry crowd surrounds someone. From the aerial footage, all I can see are shoulders and the tops of heads swarming over a spot where someone has, by now, probably stopped moving.

"I smell smoke!" someone screams, running into the waiting room.

I turn back and see, in the chairs, what looks like my sister as a child. She's squirming in one of the chairs while Mama, belly swollen, rocks back and forth, eyes squeezed shut in pain. A broad-shouldered man in dark slacks and suspenders holds her hand, or, rather, lets her squeeze his.

"Somebody shut that damn TV off!" Mama shouts. To the man, "Brother Harvey, I ain't lettin' them cut me open. Not this time. God, I just want this baby to be born." There's a nurse in front of her who keeps glancing back at the doors to the hospital operating rooms and who keeps saying, "Any time now" like some kind of mantra. Like she's forgotten how to say anything else.

"Ella, is that . . ." I trail off.

She takes a step toward the cluster of people, and I follow her, and suddenly we're outside where the chaos hits me in hi-def. A gray Cadillac races toward Florence and Normandie, and it's dusky out, but this place looks familiar. Feels familiar. I've been here before. The car skids to a stop. The man behind the wheel flicks the safety off a gun and hops out. A woman jumps out the passenger's side and runs with him to a row of stores being looted.

Helicopter blades whip overhead. Spotlights sweep the streets and sidewalks.

A rig rolls to a stop at the intersection, country music lolling out of the open windows, heard faintly through the rioting, then a piece of the mob breaks off and tears the truck door open, hauling the driver out. Rocks and chunks of concrete smash the windshield. Someone darts forward and swings down with a hammer, and the truck driver crumples.

Ella's walk is stately. I can't stop staring at the beating and the smashing and the hurting. I lose her, then run to where I last saw her. People are passing around a bottle of Olde English 800, rapping N.W.A. lyrics, some of them twisting the words of Negro spirituals to fit the rhythms. There's no police.

There's another swarm around a lone car. I get there just as a Korean woman is being dragged out by her hair. The whoop-whoop of police sirens sound as the black-and-white screeches to a stop. Two officers jump out, guns drawn, and there's a moment of hesitation before rocks and bricks arc in a storm toward them. Then they're gone.

Someone takes a near-empty bottle of Olde English left on the floor, folds up an issue of *Vibe* magazine, lights it, and hurls it at a nearby corner store. Kids nearly run me over on stolen bikes. Further down the block, guys with red and blue bandannas tied around their faces take crowbars to a pawnshop and a group of them dash in, then come out half a minute later, draped in jewelry and carrying the guns they got from the back.

A woman struggles past me burdened with toilet paper on her back and bags of kid's shoes on both arms.

I move to follow her, and I'm back in the hospital room. Mama is screaming something fierce while nurses scramble around her. A doctor breaks her water, but there's no progress. Then he and a nurse hook her up to a drip for Pitocin. I track the contractions in the changes in her face, and it's like her features are sinking even deeper into her skin from the pain. I've never heard screaming like this.

The doctor looks back and forth between Mama and the screen where I'm supposed to be showing, then shakes his hands and takes what looks like a pair of spoons and reaches into Mama beneath her gown. He fumbles around, then gives up. On the screen, I'm still not moving.

I've lost Ella, and when I rush for the hospital room door, I stumble out onto the corner of Martin Luther King and Vermont. Above me, National Guardsmen perch on roofs with their M16s aimed at the crowds, and looters hug the sides of buildings. It's late afternoon, and this can't be for real if time is moving this fast and what about Mama where's Mama?

In deserted parts of the city where the violence has abated, taxicabs pull up and keep the meters running while their riders hop out and come back with VCRs.

Smoke rises in columns over the city. I run farther, past overturned police cars and roadblocks. I have to get back to Mama. Time runs as fast as I do, and when I blink and stop running, Centinela Hospital looms over me. Night has fallen. Over a bullhorn, an official-sounding voice announces a curfew. Sirens wail as ambulance vans make a regular circuit up to and out from the hospital's main entrance. Those who walked, weak from gunshots or stabbings or dehydration or beatings or weary from having lost everything, stagger toward the doors for treatment.

Far back, I see a car stop. A two-door. And a man in dreadlocks gets out. Dark, angular face. Some of the bones still twisted in the memory of a beating. He looks at the city, looks at me, with horror. And . . . guilt. That face looks so familiar, then I nearly fall over when I realize who it is, and he's staring right at me.

"Is this my fault?" Rodney King seems to mouth at the mass streaming into the hospital. He snaps out of his trance, then gets back in his car and drives away.

Mama.

I shove my way past people who don't notice me into a waiting room filled to bursting. Blood stains the linoleum floor in pools. I crash through another set of doors, calling out "Mama! Mama!" and look into each room for Mama and Ella and me. Nothing here. I find the stairs and run up and it's on the second floor that I find them and, through the door's glass, I see Mama in her hospital gown, sweating a waterfall into the hospital's bedsheets while child-Ella looks curiously at the squirming new baby in Mama's arms. Mama's face is loose. Like how it would get when I used to catch her watching me and Ella play in that cramped Harlem apartment. It's slackened, wrung out. Liberated.

"This is how you were born," Ella says at my side.

"Why are you showing me this?" Something deep in me has cracked. I feel myslf slipping, then I land with a thud on my bed. Ella stands over me.

"This is what made you."

"Ella, please, stop." I have my head in my hands. My head is pounding. My arm is on fire. "Ella, please. Make it stop."

"It will never stop." Her voice sounds so distant, far-away, even though she's standing right in front of me. I feel like if I were to look up, I wouldn't recognize her face. What did this to her? "This. It will happen again. And again. And again. It already has."

"What do you want me to do?" I scream.

In the silence that follows, I'm huffing. Sweating. Shaking. I can't stop shaking. Whatever cracked is getting more broken, and I need to put it back together. I know I need to put it back together. I'm struggling to put it back together, but it's like I've got my shoulder pressed against a screen door in the middle of a flood. My body strains. I know what she wants. I know what she wants, but I can't give it to her. I won't.

"Ella," I tell her through gritted teeth, "I can't afford to be angry anymore. I can't. I don't have it in me to keep being this angry."

Ella kneels down so we're eye to eye. "Did you ever stop being angry?" she asks me, softly but with Mama's sternness.

"But my life," I say to her, and she knows without me saying that I mean my job and my house. She knows I mean not having my back on fire from tension, walking up and down the walkways of Rikers waiting to defend against harm. She knows I mean the fact that I haven't seen a white person since I got here. "I can't see 'em to hate 'em. Please don't take me back out there."

"Kev, it was never just 'out there.' It's here, too."

And that's when she shows me the metal Miguel and Royce and Marlon and Mero and I have been working on, have been bending, building. Shows me that it doesn't just go to damaged workers in the factory but that it's being put on cops outside to increase their reflexes, to upgrade them. That those misshapen pieces of metal we're forming make shields on their bones, beneath their skin, so that no bullet can kill them. We're building the turrets mounted on our street corners. We're working to make the police invincible.

"You were never free."

My thumb is on fire. Ella looks at me with this pained, sorrowful gaze, watches me hold my hand and try to bear the hurt. And I close my eyes and grit my teeth against the hot needles piercing every inch of skin on my thumb where that fucking chip is, and it gets bigger and bigger, the pain, until I'm blind with it, the whole world white, then it stops.

There's an arc of blood splashed in a single line down one wall. My thumb is cut open. And there on the rug in front of me, past Ella's ghost, is the chip. Glowing blue in the near-darkness.

"You took it out," I say between heavy breaths.

"No. You did." She's smiling when she says it.

Instinct tells me I should be afraid. That this is the same as cutting off my ankle monitor. They can't watch my bloodstream anymore, can't see if I'm sleeping right, can't inject compliance into my veins when I get angry, can't tell me when curfew is, can't pay me my wages, can't get me into my home, can't see me—

She touches me and there's weight in my arms, a warmth. It smells of milk. A baby.

Ella shows me. Shows me the doctors who looked down on Mama, this woman they were supposed to care for, with such disdain. With such disgust. Feeding her the wrong medicine. They didn't care whether she lived or died. Whether her child lived or died. Our sister.

Ella's looking at her. "This child could have seen the world. But they killed our sister before she even had a chance to breathe."

The weight vanishes. I can't move. "I don't want—I just want to go home."

"There is no home." Ella is gentle. "Mama prayed we would happen," she tells me. "God is a loving God, but he's also the architect of our revenge. He delivers us from

Egypt. But he also brings the locusts and the frogs and the rivers of blood."

All this time, I'd wanted it. Somewhere in the back of my mind. As a kid in those interrogation rooms, as an older kid in Rikers. Then it gets beaten out of me, and I'm convinced we're too small for it, Ella's too small for it, for burning it all down.

Is this what Ella's been doing while away?

"I can see the future, Kev," she says quietly.

I breathe deeply. Against every instinct, I say, "Show me."

She puts a hand to my head, skin against skin.

Fire and blood and screaming and singing. Shattered chunks of marble littering park grounds. Monuments to the Confederates pulverized into dust. Police stations turned into husks, watch posts unmanned and creaking with rust. Cities, whole cities, rising into the sky. So much death, but there's joy in it.

Apocalypse sweeps the South. Vengeance visits the North.

When she lets go, I'm trembling.

"Now, you can see it too," she tells me. She sticks her hand out, and I shake myself back into the present. "Tell me what you see," Ella whispers into my ear.

I see the After.

Grassland, hills that undulate, green everywhere,

except when there's fire coming out of the ground and when craters appear and the new government men knock on doors to order newly poor whites to leave, condemn houses or purchase title. The first orange and white and red fire, that time the local trash dump bursts open, is, for them, the beginning of the end. Streaks, fingers almost blue as the anthracite underground creeps closer to the surface and the asphalt is hot to the touch. The air rancid, everybody coughing, always coughing. One day, a house gets emptied, first of its things, then of its people, and a big red slash gets painted on the front door, marking it for condemnation. From the hilltop, the town is nothing but a mouth with just a few broken teeth left. They'll feel us in every corner of this country.

Then and only then will we clear those forty acres of poison, pull the radiation out of the air. Use our Thing, jettison it into space, make the land ready for our people.

"What do you see?" she says.

There's so much. It's a jumble in my head, but Ella and I are in the scorched middle of it.

"Freedom," I tell her. "I see freedom."

ACKNOWLEDGMENTS

This book, like its title character, saw a fiery birth. Formerly a swirl of disembodied phrases and feelings and half-characters, the story of Ella and Kev began to coalesce while, in Paris, I learned of the non-indictments of the police officers responsible for the deaths of Michael Brown and Eric Garner. After the revelation of the circumstances surrounding the shooting death of Laquan McDonald, I began to hear, with greater force, the stirrings of Ella's voice and Kev's. Each new horrifically regular death, whether upon initial police contact or later during police or carceral custody, made clearer what I wanted to say. Because while I mourned, I thought of the families left behind and how the orbit of hurt at the center of which sits each of these tragedies is spread almost beyond imagining. In a fiction genre that traffics in the impossible, I wondered how such people, such families, might find themselves situated.

What might the opposite of injustice look like?

My fearless, peerless editor at Tor.com Publishing, Ruoxi

Chen, helped turn my questions and convictions into this book. Its fiercest advocate, she challenged me like I'd never been challenged before to write my way into a story that at times seemed beyond my abilities to tell. From the beginning, she saw this book, saw more of it than I could. To say that working with her has been a dream would be to indulge in criminal understatement. Our Gchats shall remain some of the most cherished and expansive conversations I've ever had the privilege and pleasure of having.

I must thank my agent, Noah Ballard, who kept me levelheaded and focused and who was ceaseless in his encouragement.

And I send my everlasting gratitude to Irene Gallo and Christine Foltzer for directing the creation of a cover that, to this day, renders me breathless. Jaya Miceli delivered one of the most stunning pieces of art I have ever seen in my life. I am the most fortunate author in the world to have been able to have my name on this cover.

My family, of course. For your steadfast belief in me pursuing this career, in which I am neither a doctor nor an engineer, I thank you from the bottom of my heart.

Finally, I must acknowledge N. K. Jemisin. Until I'd read her Broken Earth trilogy, I did not know how to write angry, the type of angry that still leaves room for love. Those books unlocked a gate. The reader in me is ever grateful.

So is the writer.